WALKING WITH
SHADOWS

D1713629

PRAISE FOR *WALKING WITH SHADOWS*

"This novel is indeed provocative in a very positive sense. It wills mankind to go deeper than the norm to search out those insecurities that hobble the quest for community"
– Uzor Maxim Uzoatu

"Dibia's debut novel is a fine and compelling work."
– Chris Dunton

Also by Jude Dibia

Blackbird

Unbridled

WALKING WITH
SHADOWS

A NOVEL

BY

JUDE DIBIA

Writers' Collective

First published in Nigeria by BlackSands Books in 2005
This edition published by Jalaa Writers' Collective
3 Ogun Street, off Mercy Eneli Street
Surulere, Lagos

Copyright © Jude Dibia, 2011

ISBN 978-1-4116-1934-0

All rights reserved

Jude Dibia has asserted his right under the Copyright, Design and
Patents Acts, 1988 to be identified as the author of this work

This novel is a work of fiction. Names and characters are the product
of the author's imagination and any resemblance to actual persons,
living or dead, is entirely coincidental

This book is sold subject to the condition that it shall not, by way of
trade or otherwise, be lent, resold, hired out, or otherwise
circulated without the publisher's prior consent in any
form of binding or cover other than that in which it
is published and without a similar condition
including this condition being imposed
on the subsequent purchaser.

www.jalaawriters.com

ABOUT THE AUTHOR

 Jude Dibia is the author of two well received novels; *Walking with Shadows* (2005) and *Unbridled* (2007). Jude's novels have been described as daring and controversial by readers and critics in and out of Africa. *Walking with Shadows* is said to be the first Nigerian novel that has a gay man as its central character and that treats his experience with great insight, inviting a positive response to his situation. *Unbridled*, too, stirred some controversy on its publication; a story that tackled the emancipation of its female protagonist who had suffered from incest and abuse from men. *Unbridled* was awarded the 2007 Ken Saro-Wiwa Prize for Prose (sponsored by NDDC/ANA) and was a finalist in the 2008 Nigeria Prize for Literature (sponsored by NLNG).

What is morality in any given time or place?
It is what the majority then and there happen to like,
and immorality is what they dislike.

– Alfred North Whitehead

PROLOGUE

Ebele was going to die today.

He knew it. He welcomed it. He was simply going to let it happen so that Adrian could be born. He only hoped it would be painless. It should be painless; after all he was surrounded by hundreds of black angels in gleaming white robes, just like him, waiting to be reborn though most of them didn't know it yet. This was a day for rebirths.

He looked ahead of the crowd and picked out his brothers, Chiedu and Chika, also in white, hands clasped together prayerfully. How innocent they looked. How Christlike!

Ebele caught a glimpse of the pastor baptising a young girl in the stream. His huge frame and unsmiling face made him more ominous than holy. He was surrounded by two junior clergymen who helped to hold the new converts in the stream while he prayed over them. His huge, hairy left hand pressed on the submerged chest, while the Bible-wielding right was raised up in celestial suspension as he screamed out prayers and banished all the evil that may have once possessed the new child of God.

The scene was so surreal to Ebele. It had taken his family about two hours that morning to drive to the small town of Ifo in Ogun State. His father had made sure they were awake as early as five, and by six they left their home in

Ikoyi. When they reached Oshodi, the usual rowdiness, the endless flood of yellow and black-striped *kombi* buses, the conductors hoarse from yelling for fares, were not there. Only a few buses operated at that early hour. The road was free and the potholes that riddled it could be seen in all their glory, as could the surrounding shanty towns harbouring many a hardened youth. There were houses here made of metal sheets only. One-room metal huts for entire families: father, mother, children. The homeless had managed to cover themselves up in tattered wraps, and now lay on the ledge of the bridge and on the pavements. They seemed to be fighting for space with the heaps of dirt piled on the street corners under signboards that warned 'No Dumping of Refuse Here.' Ebele and his brothers lived a privileged life in the suburb of Ikoyi, and their reality was very different from this one. In Ikoyi the roads were smooth. There were green lawns and functioning streetlights. In the early morning, ladies in uniformed overcoats came out to sweep the streets and pick up the rubbish thrown out of moving cars. Ebele could not remember seeing homeless people there.

When his father took a sharp turning to the left of the bad road, it seemed they had entered yet another world. Here there was red earth and plenty vegetation. The houses were different too: sparse, mud huts, cemented but unpainted blockhouses with raffia or rusty, thin metal roofs. Each open compound had fruit trees and stray animals – local dogs, goats, chickens – running around.

After about another thirty minutes of driving through this village, the family passed a tollgate which announced their arrival in Ogun State. Their father wound down his window to pay the fare. When he did this, a throng of street vendors rushed to the car and thrust their goods in his face:

"Daddy, buy my bread, e dey sweet and fresh."

"Buy groundnut, ti-rii for five naira…"

"Mummy, I give you good price for my plantain chips."

Ebele was not the least interested in their wares, however, his eyes was fixed on one of the vendors. He was a young man, probably in his early twenties, dressed in a simply off-white singlet and torn jeans. He hawked newspapers. Ebele was drawn to the fine line of his silhouette as he shoved the other sellers aside and tried to be ahead of the pack. He thrust a paper to the window closest to Ebele. The 'Daily Times of Nigeria' in arresting red captured Ebele's attention. It was his father's favourite newspaper. The date was beneath, Saturday, June 5, 1982. Ebele read it all, even before his eys settled on the finer prints that announced the newspaper's founding year.

Ebele's father brushed all the sellers aside with one big sweep of his hand and screamed at them to leave his car. It wasn't long after that before the family reached the Ifo stream. It was magical and pristine. The hundreds of people waiting to be baptised in their spotless white robes contrasting with the greens of the trees and shrubs, the red and brown of the earth, and the glistening shine of the awakening, sun-kissed stream, were a sight to behold.

This was a good-enough day to be reborn, and Ebele could not have chosen a better location himself. His ten-year-old mind was in a hurry to rid itself of the pathetic person it had always known as 'Ebele.' He looked again at the long chain of people ahead of him and found himself reciting in his heart:

Ringa-Ringa-Roses
A-Pocket-Full-of-Posies…

He loved that game, the running around in circles, singing and chasing his shadow. But he had been told that he was not supposed to like it. It was not a manly game and he was often laughed at when he played with the girls. After today he would never play the game again. He would be a new person.

Soon, he was at the foot of the stream and it was his turn to be baptised, for Ebele to fade away and die. The pastor motioned for him to come forward and Ebele slowly entered the stream, stopping in front of the clergymen. In panic, he realised that the water level was just above his stomach. He could not swim; he could drown, he thought. Stupid. Of course he wouldn't; that was why the two junior clergymen were there, to hold on to him while he was lowered into the water.

"What patron saint have you chosen to be named after?" the pastor demanded.

"Saint Adrian," Ebele answered in a whisper.

"*Saint Adrian?!*" The pastor was bewildered.

"Yes, sir."

The burly man considered Ebele for a minute longer before he started praying. He took hold of Ebele and slowly lowered him into the water. Submerging deep, Ebele felt the hands of the men grip him to prevent a struggle, and again he became panic-stricken.

He closed his eyes tightly. He believed that if he closed his eyes tight enough, it would happen. Ebele would fade away and Adrian would emerge.

Yes, he would close his eyes and keep them tightly shut. In the fuzzy red and black darkness behind his eyelids, he could only hear the rushing flow of the stream and faintly make out the sound of the pastor's voice in prayer. He panicked again. This felt long. Was this the same amount of time the others were submerged in the stream? Was it only his imagination that he had been in there longer than the others?

He gave up these thoughts as he felt himself truly fading away. He was not going to resist the drowning sensation; he simply was going to let himself go. It was like falling asleep at the bottom of the sea…

1

He was slowly coming awake. His head was still hurting and, for a brief moment, he was lost, unsure where he was. His eyes opened and the blur in front of him cleared up. He was in his car. The car was in a ditch by an intersection. There were other cars parked close by. A small crowd of people were gathered around his car, staring into it. Instinctively, he gazed at the clock on the dashboard: 19:21. He had left his office only ten minutes earlier. He remembered he had been racing down the highway when a rickety water tanker shot in from nowhere. He had swerved to avoid a collision. He looked up and caught a glimpse of the same tanker parked in front of his car.

He was all right except for the pain in his head and the throbbing of a swelling on his forehead. He touched it and jumped when someone forced the car door open and tried pulling him out of it. He struggled. Ten minutes before now, his world as he knew it was going to be destroyed. He was rushing off to make sure he told her before anyone else did. Before she heard it from the wrong people. There was nothing he could do to change what was going to happen, but he was certainly going to come clean with it all. Somehow, it was a bit of a relief.

The crowd around his car were saying things. He could not hear but had the vague feeling that they were trying to communicate with him. His eyes were drawn to a frail, hungry-looking old man who kept pleading with his eyes and indeed every part of his untidy body, and pointing to the truck. The driver, he guessed. He had to go, he had to get home. He had to tell her.

"I'm okay. Thank you."

"Sorry sir," the tanker driver said in shaky English, "I no see you on time."

"I'm ok," he kept on saying, "I have to go."

What is my name? He asked his inner being. Everything was confusing now. He searched his wallet for his driver's licence. It was there. *Ebele Njoko. Adrian Njoko.* Yes, that was it, Adrian. Adrian had to get home. He shut his door again, started his car and was glad when the engine responded. Ignoring the dozen odd people gathered around him, he backed up his Mercedes-Benz C-Class and drove off.

He was not a rude man, but he was preoccupied. It had started with a phone call at the office and then the harsh reality hit him. He was going to lose his family. He was going to lose his life; a life that had taken him a long time to build. What had he been thinking all those years? The sheer guilt of living a lie for so long pricked him. But he had gone straight, suppressed a lot of feelings and had even denied himself so much and now this, that one phone call that was to change his life.

" You bastard!… I am going to tell them."

He had broken out in a cold sweat after that call. It rattled him. He knew exactly what it meant and he knew he had put off facing this moment for a long time now. He slowed down a notch and took a right turn that led directly to a side street. He was nearly there. It took him exactly five more minutes to get to the front of a black gate in the exclusive housing estate. House 19H.

He sat still in his car sweating profusely. Without

thinking, he placed his head on the steering wheel and let out a silent sigh. *Why am I so nervous? Why am I such a wreck?*

After what seemed like forever, he got out of the car. He walked slowly to the gate and nudged it a little. The gate creaked open slowly but noisily. There was no one waiting to greet him. There was an eerie silence that was unsettling and, at that moment, it struck him that he might be too late. The compound was not a very big one, but it was neat and took two cars with a little play space for a child or two. Walking up the three steps that led to the front door, Adrian felt a nervous squeeze in his heart, and a dizzy spell overcame him. He paused at the entrance of the house for just a second before he grabbed the door handle and pushed his way into the foyer that led directly into the living room.

Even from where he stood he could see her. Her reflection on the huge decorative mirror by the side table was still. She did not react to his entrance. It was like she was in deep thought or even hypnotised. She only moved when he had fully entered the room and was standing in front of her. She smiled. It was a forced and painful look and underneath it Adrian could see traces of tears playing hide-and-seek in the shadows of her eyes.

"Adrian, you are back early," she said almost in a whisper.

Adrian remained silent. What words could he utter?

"I had the strangest phone call today," she continued. "I'm so confused Adrian, it all did not make sense."

"Ada, where is Ego?" Adrian asked for their daughter. "She's not here."

"She's at Amaka's house down the street," Ada replied softly. She stood up abruptly and was looking at his hands and the swelling on his forehead. "Where are your office things? Laptop, jacket."

"In the car," Adrian said in reply. "You said you had a phone call, what was it about?" He was worried. He had never seen his wife act this calmly before. Normally she was the over-excited type, almost hyperactive. Something was very different now. He had seen the tears in her eyes. She must have been crying earlier.

"It was a man." Ada spoke slowly, and then her features hardened. "He claimed… I don't understand what he was trying to say…" She trailed off but kept her eyes fixed on Adrian's.

"What did he say?" Adrian demanded.

"I had to send Ego off to her friend's place after that," she continued, "I couldn't bear to let her see me cry… Not that I cried, but I was so confused and then angry and…"

She kept on talking, the words tumbling out in torrents. Her eyes were wide and wild with questions seeking truths or untruths, just anything to make them all right again.

"You haven't told me what he said," Adrian insisted.

"Is it true?" Ada asked, tears rolling down her cheeks. "Apart from me, have you been with another one… another *man*?"

When she said *"man,"* it was in a low murmur forced out of her breath. Her eyes held his with desperation, pleading for him to say it was all a lie. At that moment she didn't know how she felt but it appeared frozen in eternity.

"Honey, there are things I must tell you," Adrian began. He tried holding her arms but she instinctively shrugged him off. His eyes momentarily drifted to the muted plasma screen television in the far corner of the living room and slowly refocused on her very beautiful but now anguished face.

"Are you gay, Adrian?" Ada asked a little too calmly. "Have you been gay all this while we've been married?"

Adrian finally looked away. His heart was beating so fiercely she must have heard it, and there was an ungodly throbbing in his head. He could almost swear that she could hear his heart beat. His legs became weak. His mouth dried up instantly making him thirsty. His breathing was short but deep. He remembered this feeling as a child when he had done something really bad and his dad would tell him to go kneel down in his room and wait for him. This was the feeling of impending punishment. But the waiting was the real punishment, not necessarily the beating to come.

"I love you Ada."

Adrian spoke quietly but Ada was shouting now. "Are you gay?"

"I was a lot of things before I met you," Adrian said. "I dabbled in all sorts before I fell in love with you. But meeting you changed a lot of things for me, and then we had Ego…"

"Are you?"

"I was!" His tone was stern, as he was little irritated that she seemed disinterested in his love for her and their daughter.

"You were?" She repeated it slowly. "You knew this and still deceived me and still married me and still had the guts to make love to me and put your thing in me!"

"Being gay was my past and when I met you all that didn't matter since it wasn't me anymore and I loved you. Honey, I never wanted you to find out about that part of my life."

Ada burst out laughing. The laugh was cynical but tinged with pain and regret. Her body rocked with the force of it, and it soon became hysterical tears. Hysterical crying hard to distinguish from laughter. She shook her head and slumped on the leather sofa. Then she held her head with her fingers and massaged her temple. This could not be happening to her, she kept thinking. She had the perfect marriage. She was the envy of her friends. She had a lovely home, a beautiful child and a caring husband with a fantastic job. How would she face the world and hold her head up proudly? How would she face her family, *his* family? How would she tell her daughter that her father was a fraud? How could she continue to live with him?

Adrian sat beside her on the sofa. He was looking at her but did not know what to say. He did love her; why couldn't she simply see that?

"What are we going to do? Why did you let me live this lie for all these years?"

"It is no lie that I love you."

"I don't want to hear that," she pleaded, closing her eyes. "So what the hell is this? Are you gay or what? You said you were…. So does that mean that you choose to be gay when it suits you?"

Adrian had not thought about that. He was gay. He knew this ever since he started having sexual urges as a child. He had realised he was different from his brothers and other boys. He knew at seven when he shared a bath with a friend spending the night, Ekene. His mum had banished them to the bathroom to clean up before dinner and, being young, there had been no problem jumping into the tub together. As they sponged each other laughing and squealing, he felt a closeness to Ekene that was not entirely platonic. He had no name for it then as a child, but as he grew up, experiencing this feeling for other boys and then men, he knew the words: homosexual, gay!

"Honey, nothing has to change. I haven't changed, we can simply continue with our lives."

"Have you gone mad? What do you mean nothing has changed? Everything has changed."

Ada stood up and began to pace the room. She could not bring herself to look at her husband. First she had to try to wipe out the mental image in her head of him and another man. How would her life ever be the same again?

She knew what she must do. She turned round and faced him.

"Who was it that called me?" She demanded. "Was that your lover?"

"What!" Adrian said. "Hell, no! It was someone in the office who just got fired... I uncovered a scam and he was involved... I have no lover Ada... I have been clean since we've been together."

Ada sniffed at his last comment. She was not interested in what he had to say about their life together. She simply had to start thinking of herself and *her* daughter. She had to start fixing up the broken pieces of her life.

"We can't be together right now. Would you rather I moved out or you did?"

"This is not necessary, Ada. I know you are upset, I understand that, but don't do this. This will destroy us, our family."

"Fine; then I'll move out with Ego." She spoke with some resolve.

"No," Adrian begged, "I'll leave, but please forgive me. We need to talk this through... Do you love me? Have you ever loved me?"

"Stop talking about love," she spat. "I just need you to get away from me and Ego... There's nothing for us to say to each other right now."

There was an uncomfortable silence. Adrian understood her anger and feeling of betrayal. But he was scared of the direction things were taking. If they became separated now, their family might not survive it. If he could only talk to her and make her understand that he loved her and that his past had been buried long before now. This was exactly what Tayo wanted. The bastard had threatened to ruin his home and career if Adrian exposed the scam in the office.

"Ada, kiss Ego for me." Adrian stood up and moved

towards the door. "I will spend the night at Chiedu's place and will call you in the morning." Chiedu was his elder brother.

Ada did not respond. She turned her back to him as he walked out of the door and, as soon as it closed behind him, she broke down again and began to cry.

◉ ◉ ◉

WORRIES FLOODED his already troubled mind as Adrian drove off. Was he on the verge of losing his family? Maybe. Had he really committed a crime for loving a woman and creating a beautiful family with her? Perhaps. What was he really being punished for? Being gay? Betraying his sexuality? Going straight? Being a committed husband and father? Exposing fraud at his workplace?

He replayed his confrontation with his wife, all the things she said… *Are you gay or what? You said you were… So does that mean that you choose to be gay when it suits you?* Ada was so crushed and he knew she had started crying again when he left. He had heard her muffled sobs from the other side of the door. He wanted to go back in and console her, but she would have just rejected him and put up a fight. She was right. They both needed some space. But he didn't want to be away from his wife, his daughter. They had become an integral part of his existence. They had been the support he had needed for years. All his life he had been afraid that he would end up alone, and they had been there to let him know that this would not happen. Now, he felt *very* alone. Abandoned. And it was scary.

He had no idea where he was driving to until he found himself in the parking lot of the huge housing complex famously christened '1004' for its number of flats. Adrian hadn't been here in six years – since he got married to be precise. The last time he had come, he had resolved never to return. It symbolised a big part of his past life, the life he was determined to forget. A flood of nostalgia washed over him briefly as he allowed himself to remember. A stifled laugh escaped his lips. It was the first time he had smiled all evening. He shook his head and got out of the car, making sure to lock the doors before proceeding to the stairs. The elevators had not worked for as far back as he could remember. He had once joked that if he ever pushed the buttons to the elevator and the doors flew open, he would run for dear life. He simply would not trust his life to that contraption. Like almost everything in the country, the people had just let everything die, just like their hopes.

The *mallam* who sold cigarettes, sweets and cheap biscuits still had a stand by the foot of the stairs. He smiled at Adrian, exposing his cola-yellowed teeth and reddened gum with black spots.

"Oga," he said, "*welcome o! E don tey since you come hia.*"

"Thank you," Adrian replied, returning the smile.

"*Lift dey work, oga,*" the *mallam* informed Adrian as he made to start the long climb to the stairs to the seventh floor.

Adrian paused for a moment. The elevator was actually working! He turned round and pushed the button and waited. Within a minute, to his surprise, the elevator opened up. He smiled again to himself and, hesitating for just a brief moment, stepped in. He had been running away for too long.

As the door closed him in and the lift started its slow ascension, Adrian's heartbeat accelerated. He wondered why he had come here, to this place. What answers was he expecting to find? A small, but persistent, voice within him kept whispering that everything would be alright. He just had to talk to somebody. He had to talk to somebody who would understand.

The elevator lurched open on the seventh floor. It had been a smooth successful ride. Adrian jumped out. Instinct carried his feet to the front door of the apartment he had once known so well. Nothing had changed. The door was still a sickening milk colour. The cranky doorbell, a relic from the 80s, was intact. The same old foot mat welcoming home. It was like the entire place refused to succumb to change. In spite of his fear, the familiarity had a soothing effect. Pulling himself together, he raised his hand and pressed the doorbell, listening to the distant "ding-dong" it made within the house.

A voice called from inside the house. "One moment!" Adrian listened as the door was unlatched and pulled open. Abdul's face was stunned.

He was the same Abdul but slightly older. His head was scraped bald like before, but this did not hide the trace of greying. He was as lean as always, elegant too, dressed now in a matching linen top and trousers with silver embroidery adorning the lapel. He was wearing his geeky but playful glasses. Abdul was a beautiful man and would always be.

"*Na wa o! Na you be dis?* Adrian Njoko! What a surprise!"

"Abdul," Adrian smiled slightly. "It's good to see you again."

Abdul still had a dazed look. It seemed he spent another five minutes just staring at Adrian, as if studying all his features to see if he had changed.

"May I come in?"

"Abeg no mind me," Abdul said stepping aside to give way to him. "Please come in… I'm just surprised."

The sweet smell of scented candles with a hint of jasmine and lavender greeted Adrian. Alas! Something had changed: the white walls and cane furniture had been replaced by terracotta red and a deep blue, a sofa, a beautiful shade of pale red, on a mahogany frame, and a petit glass coffee table supported by a delicate, sculpted wrought-iron base. The windows were covered with a seemingly endless stream of peach-coloured voile. Dotting the walls were paintings from local artists. Knick-knacks from foreign trips stood on the display shelf in the corner. There were miniature masks from Ethiopia, snow-globes, carvings from South Africa and other odd little objects.

"Please take a seat," Abdul offered. "Wow! What a surprise!… It's been what, five, six years?"

"Six," Adrian confirmed as he sat down on one of the comfy chairs adjacent to the huge sofa.

"You've added some weight. That wife of yours must be treating you well. How is she?"

The silence was deafening. The smile on Abdul's face slowly vanished. Something was wrong. He could sense it. This visit wasn't a mere social call.

With an exaggerated show of excitement Abdul suddenly sprang up. "Where are my manners? What should I offer you to drink?"

"I'm fine," Adrian said. "How have you been? Are you still with…"

"Femi?" Abdul completed his question. "Yes I am. He should be back from work soon."

Adrian smiled to himself. These two had been the longest-going gay couple he knew. They had been together for about ten years already.

"Can't believe you're still together," Adrian admitted. "How do you handle the gossip, disapproving looks, et cetera?"

Abdul lit a cigarette and offered one to Adrian, who declined. He had stopped smoking years earlier, after Ada.

"People will always talk and gossip," Abdul said wisely. "I love myself and my life, and I love Femi. This is all that matters. Of course, I don't go about advertising the fact that

I'm *'queer'*. I don't expect the average heterosexual man to rub his sexuality in my face, so I don't expect he expects me to rub mine in his."

Adrian replied quickly. "That's a double standard and you know it Abdul, I don't believe you buy into that."

"No, maybe I don't, but I refuse to be a hypocrite when it comes to these matters. The heterosexuals rub their *ye-ye* sexuality in our faces daily. It's right there when you open the glossy magazines and see all the colourful adverts for clothes, perfume, everything. It's on the billboards, the television, radio, everywhere, and no one objects, not least the gay folks. But if I were to hold hands with Femi in public, *na another story be dat one…* This doesn't mean I should stoop to their level by advertising my sexuality. I don't need their validation or approval, Adrian."

"Then whose do you need?"

Abdul took a long drag from his cigarette and exhaled a thin cloud of smoke. There was amusement in his eyes. He knew this game they were playing; he had played out this very one with Adrian a long time before when he was searching for answers. He wouldn't mind doing it again. Something was indeed troubling his old friend.

"The people that matter in my life," Abdul simply said. "My dad died two years ago, Adrian, and he never knew anything about me. His knowing might have killed him earlier, who knows? I was his first son and he saw no grandchild from me. After his death I decided to let my family know, so they wouldn't have to wait indefinitely for me to bring a wife to them, and a child. Also, I had to release my younger ones… none of them could marry until I did – some traditional stuff we practise. Anyway, I got really sick of the life I had, the lying, and the hiding. It was killing me. I had to tell them. So I did."

"And what happened?" Adrian sat up straight. He had

never heard any part of this before. It had been some time, after all, since they last saw or spoke to each other.

"My mum cried. But I don't know if she was crying because she had lost her husband or that she was not to expect a grandchild from me. But later, she told me she had always known. I didn't ask her how or when she knew."

"And your siblings?"

Abdul only shrugged.

"After that, I felt free," he announced. "Come on Adrian, I know you too well. You didn't come to see me years after you decided to keep away, just to discuss me… Something has happened to you… Something upsetting!"

Adrian looked away. He was debating how best to tell his old friend. A feeling of betrayal lurked in his heart. Also he dreaded the familiar *"I told you so!"* situations like this prompted. But looking again into Abdul's eyes, he detected no sign of triumph or accusation, only love and understanding.

So he blurted it out. "Ada knows about me."

Abdul did not speak at first. It was eery. The murmuring of the air conditioner in one of the bedrooms was audible, and the *drip-drip-drip* of a leaking tap somewhere, probably in the kitchen, began to grate on Adrian's nerves…

"What happened?" Abdul finally asked after a small eternity. "How did she find out?"

Adrian narrated everything to him: the fraud he had exposed at his office and how Tayo Onasanya, one of the culprits, had threatened to tell everybody, including his family. He told Abdul of how he had met Ada at home and how she had asked him to leave.

"How did this Tayo know about you?"

"One of my South African colleagues let it slip by mistake once, while they were having lunch. Judith, that is her name, is gay as well and tells everybody who cares to know. It happened so long ago and Tayo never confronted me with the knowledge of it."

"Have you spoken to anyone else in your family?"

"No."

Abdul stood up and walked over to the remote control of the mute television, picked it up and switched off the TV. He lit another cigarette and again offered Adrian the pack. Again, Adrian waved him off.

"Let's put things into perspective first. Your wife knows you *were* gay, and probably other members of your family know by now. What is the worst thing that can happen next?"

"What do you mean *'what's the worst thing that can happen?'* Adrian asked with some irritation. "How will I face my family? I don't want to lose my wife and kid."

Abdul stared at him after his last statement. The look in his eyes was not friendly either. It showed disappointment and a hint of anger. But when he finally spoke, his voice betrayed no such thing.

"You sound like you are ashamed of your past. You sound like you had a choice in determining your sexuality… You sound like it is a curse to be homosexual and you should be punished for your crimes."

Adrian understood the depth of what his friend was saying. But the truth was he did feel ashamed of himself, but not for the same reasons that Abdul was thinking.

"If you feel so strongly about your guilt, then maybe you deserve to lose your family after all," Abdul added rather harshly. He hadn't meant for it to come out like that.

"Don't say that. I'm so confused right now. I didn't want anybody to get hurt because of me."

"And how many times would you allow other people to hurt you?" Abdul moved closer to Adrian, dropping a warm hand on his shoulder.

"I don't understand," Adrian admitted.

"Every day in a gay man's life, he is constantly hurt by the people he loves the most. His family. His friends. And even society. We have to live with rejection every day and that hurts. We have to *grin and bear it* constantly so that other people are comfortable at our expense." Abdul took a deep breath. "What I'm trying to say is, you can't help but hurt people you love sometimes. The only difference here is you are conscious of it. Most people are not, or simply don't care."

Adrian remained silent as he pondered Abdul's speech.

"But you have your fault here," Abdul added. "You are right to feel guilty because you did deceive your wife. You are gay Adrian…always are, always will be. You shouldn't have married a woman. I did warn you."

There, he said it. Abdul thought back to their last conversation when he had tried to make Adrian see some sense. He also remembered Adrian's reply then. Even as the years passed, he had hoped that things would be different for Adrian and that he would remain happy. He had hoped that his life would take a different path from all the others before him who became weak and abandoned their families.

"What do I do now?" Adrian whispered almost to himself.

"I can't tell you what to do. But you must be true to yourself, for once in your life. If you can only think of what the worst thing is that can happen, then you will be fine. Your friends will always be your friends. Your family will learn to love you for who you are and life will go on."

Adrian knew he was right, and it helped to hear it said, but this did not wipe away his sense of dread. And long after he left 1004, he still could not shut out the niggling voices in his head.

2

With a start, Ada realized she had been sitting in the same spot since Adrian left, for the last hour and a half, in a trancelike haze. Her tears had dried up leaving her with nothing, even if she had wanted to cry some more. She just sat there staring at the wall in front of her, which had become colourless, empty, invisible.

It was true what her mother used to say jokingly, that in times of deep personal crisis, your entire lifespan runs through your mind in a split second. It was so true! She had seen herself as a toddler; as a young child protesting whenever she had to have her hair done in cornrows; as a budding teenager full of life and promise; her wedding day; the first time she lost her innocence. It all merged in one swift motion.

Adrian was a Nigerian, an African man. Being gay was certainly not in African culture. The whole idea was so foreign, so unnatural. But while everyone knew it existed, the probability it would be so close to home was one she would never have imagined. There had been people in school she suspected of being gay, and she had always believed she was tolerant of their lifestyle and sexual choices. She could hardly call herself tolerant now! Now that it was her reality.

But was she blind? How could she have missed all the signs? Had she simply allowed herself to see only what she wanted to see? How could she have missed it all? The deeper she reflected, the more questions she uprooted like stubborn weed.

She was distracted by the noise of the front door flying open. She turned round to see Isioma, the housemaid, leading Ego into the living room. Ego yanked her little plump arm away from Isioma and dashed head first towards Ada with great speed. She dived and squealed.

"Mummy!"

Ada almost tossed her aside in shock when she caught the delightful look in her young baby eyes. They were Adrian's eyes. Ego had his colour, his chin and even his hair. It was too much for Ada, as if Adrian was in front of her once again, now taunting her in the image of their daughter; a reminder that he would always remain a part of her life.

"Mummy!" Ego screamed as she fell off the sofa and landed with a thud on the marble floor. "Mummy, mummy, mummy!" she cried out continuously.

"My baby!" Ada screamed too as she made a grab for her.

Ego's raised arms clasped hers and soon they both were locked in an embrace, both crying.

"Aunty," Isioma called out in worry, "let me go and bathe Ego!"

By now Isioma was standing in Ada front waiting to carry the child away, but Ada shook her head and gestured that she should leave. Hesitating only momentarily, Isioma turned and headed for the kitchen. In the silence that followed, Ada reflected on what she had just done. She had literally pushed her daughter away because of her striking resemblance to her father. What kind of a mother was she? She had hurt her little darling without thinking. She squeezed a little tighter and felt her daughter's sobs abating.

"How's my baby?" Ada cooed into her ears.

"Fine, mummy." The four-year-old pushed her head away from her mother's bosom. "I had ice cream at Amaka's house and we played the piano... I played 'Mary Had a Little Lamp' and Amaka's mummy said I was very good."

"You are the best!" Ada insisted. "Now, go meet Isioma and tell her to give you a bath, okay?"

"OK, mummy." Ego slid down her mother. "Mummy, what about daddy?

"Daddy will be back soon," Ada lied. "Go and meet Isioma."

Ego stared at her mother uncertainly before she turned and walked away.

Once again, Ada was engulfed and overwhelmed by silence. She still hadn't thought about what she was eventually going to do. They had been such a perfect couple to the outside world. They were the perfect couple up till that very morning. Whom could she talk to about this? How would she even begin to tell anyone about it? In fact she certainly could not tell anyone, not her family. She wouldn't be able to bear the sympathy and the shame of it all. Yes, shame. This was *her* shame. Her very own private misery. She could not let anyone share in it.

Where had she gone wrong? She asked herself this question, secretly knowing the answer. But she had closed that door years earlier. She didn't want to revisit that old place, that old truth, that old compromise! The signs had certainly been there. Adrian was a pretty man, gentle in spirit, with an elegant gait. She once told him he walked funny, a calculated yet animated strut. He spoke with such elegance and polish. His hair was always in place, always perfect. His eyebrows a perfect bow. His mustache eternally trimmed. The twinkle in his eyes when he laughed! His voice? Soft and musical.

Never marry a pretty boy, especially one prettier than you. A friend had once advised her after a chance meeting with Adrian. *They always have a dark secret or are so conceited.*

Adrian was so immaculately neat. He was always arranging things and had all the best ideas for doing up the house. Those subtle signs and she had totally ignored them, even when her spirits had whispered to her.

Ada's roaming eyes rested on their wedding picture on a mantle by the entertainment unit. Even then she knew something. How could she not have? No! She stopped herself from thinking in that direction. She just couldn't.

But she couldn't stop her thoughts from wandering back in time. Back to when they had first met eight years before, back to Nkechi's party. Nkechi was her slightly older cousin from her father's side of the family. People always confused them for sisters. But Nkechi was much prettier, though they shared the same light-skinned complexion and stature: slim but not so tall.

It was the harmattan of 1997. Christmas was only nine days away and Nkechi was throwing a little thing to mark her thirtieth birthday, or rather her husband Obi was throwing a party for his pregnant wife. Ada, who had just finished with university and was in Lagos for the holidays, was enjoying a well-deserved break from Jos, where she was posted for her Youth Service. But she had come for other reasons as well. Nkechi had promised to introduce her to one of her colleagues at work.

"I swear you will simply love him. He's adorable and single."

"So why didn't you marry him yourself then?" Ada had teased back.

But she hadn't been disappointed when she met Adrian. He wasn't exactly her type. He was rather quiet with a sweet smile. She had avoided him for the better part of the evening, making sure she was too busy helping with serving the guests, but stealing long glances from the kitchen door. He was indeed cute, but there was also something unnerving about his every move. Something deliberate. It was apparent when he crossed his legs. It was there again when he lit a cigarette and held it between his fingers, and while taking a drag on it. Everything about him appeared perfect. That was what unnerved her most. She liked her men a little rough around the edges and not so pretty.

Before the night was over they had a chance to chat and exchange numbers. Adrian promised to call and he had, and so began their unusual courtship. Unusual, because she seemed to be the one responsible for sustaining the relationship. She had no choice, as her type of men were not interested in her. Everyone admitted she was a beauty. Light-skinned with natural long hair, petit and shapely. But for some reason, she just wasn't attracting men. She was not one to hang out at night in clubs. The truth was, her upbringing forbade it Wherever she was, she had to be home by seven or else her dad would ground her. Her parents were strict. No boys in the house, no boys on the phone and no late nights. She hadn't developed any good social skills to help her in the men department. Now as a graduate, she found herself emotionally challenged when it came to meeting the opposite sex.

Nkechi knew this much about Ada and that was why she had helped engineer her meeting Adrian. It worked, kind of, with some hiccups. Like, he hardly ever called. She had to make sure they spoke to each other every day if possible. Adrian always had excuses for not calling. He was ever so busy. It was as if he lacked genuine interest. She should have cut loose before things grew, but at the same time she found his nonchalance a tad sexy. Maybe it was true that women were attracted to men who had no regard for them. Or was it that she was so desperate to be in love with someone and be loved back that she was ready to compromise on almost everything? She was ready to be blind and see only what she wanted to see. And what was it she wanted to see? The perfect man! An escape from her boring existence! Independence from her family!

Was she blind simply out of her own selfish need? If this was true, who had deceived whom? Did she love Adrian from the beginning or had she just learned to over time?

The squeal of delight coming from the bedroom brought Ada back to the present. It was Ego. Her sweet baby! Would she ever be able to tell her the truth? What could she say and how?

This is my private grief, Ada repeatedly told herself. She wondered how she was going to go on. She hadn't thought it all through. Would she remain married to Adrian? Would they share the same house, the same bed? Would she need to have an AIDS test done? And was her daughter in danger too?

A cold fear gripped her now. She had never in her life considered the reality of AIDS or HIV, but the truth was she had been at risk for all these years. What if Adrian was still sleeping with other men while they were married? Was this possible? He had clearly said that he *was* gay, but no longer so. Could she take his word for it? After all, he had lied to her for eight years. Why should she trust him now?

All those trips to London, Abuja, New York in the guise of work could have been opportunities for him to meet other men. Adrian had hardly ever been apart from them, except when he went on his business trips. Ada tried to tell herself to stop thinking this way but she was scared. She needed to start making plans. First thing in the morning, she would take both herself and Ego to the hospital for an HIV test. What reason would she give the curious doctors and nurses? She owed no one any explanation. It was just a routine check. A confident smile and a nonchalant attitude would get her through that ordeal.

This was just crazy. She couldn't believe that there was even a slight possibility that she was infected. She remembered the first time with Adrian. He was her first. She had been so nervous though looking forward to finally making love. They had come close many times, but then she would picture her parents and imagine what they would say if they were to find out. She believed that after sex a woman would be branded with the stains of the act. Sex would be imprinted on her and people would be able to smell it. She believed she would even walk differently, giving herself away. Her young mind had been programmed like this, which was quite ridiculous as she was educated. Yet no amount of school could erase a lifetime of the dread inspired by her parents' warnings about sex. Then there was the risk of pregnancy. She had been impressed, then, that Adrian was able to wait till their wedding day. Should she have known then? What blue-blooded male would wait that long? Even she he had secretly hoped that he would have at least insisted sooner on making love to her. She would have let him. She wanted him to be more aggressive, more man. But he had been the perfect gentleman. Should she have known then?

How could she have known though, when their first encounter had been so perfect? Adrian was gentle with her body and had brought her to climax repeatedly. All her inhibitions were discarded as soon as he took her in his arms and kissed them away. He was so gentle, so attentive, almost like he knew her body even better than she did. Only a woman would know another woman's body that well and with such precision. Was that the key? Should she have known then?

Brrrrrrrrring…brrrrrrrrring… The phone rang. Ada turned

to look at the phone on a side stool by the mantelpiece. Isioma was still in the bedroom, probably dressing Ego. Ada stood up and walked over to where the phone was placed, thinking it was probably Adrian. The thought made her uncertain about answering the call. *Brrrrrrrrring....* Instinctively, she reached out and picked up the receiver.

"Hello!" It came out as a whisper.

"Darling is that you...Ada?" the voice said. "This is Iheoma. How now?"

"Iheoma, hi! I hope everything is okay?"

"I'm fine. You didn't call me as you promised. We've not had any opportunity to plan what we are wearing to the wedding on Saturday, and is your husband coming with us?"

Ada sighed quietly. She had totally forgotten about the wedding and calling Iheoma to finalize their plans. It was the last thing on her mind after recent events. On the other hand, Iheoma was certainly not the kind of person you could ignore or simply forget to call back. But right now, Ada wished she hadn't picked up the phone. She was too preoccupied to possibly think of chatting about wedding plans with her friend. Her life was at a standstill and she couldn't deal with anything else but her grief.

"I don't think I'll be going for the wedding, Iheoma," Ada let slip as soon as Iheoma had stopped talking.

"I beg, don't start now, Ada," Iheoma said with an accusing tone. "What will Sandra think if you are not there? We are her girls, we simply must be there."

"Something has come up," Ada said. "Family stuff... I don't know."

Iheoma sensed something was wrong. Instinctively, she knew it had to do with Ada and her husband. She remained quiet for a moment wondering what exactly the problem was.

"Do you want to talk about it?" Iheoma asked, concern marking her words.

There was a pause. Ada was tempted to open up to her; after all Iheoma was a single mother. She had never married the father of her child and had braved the stigma of being looked upon as a loose woman. She has even survived the disapproval of her family.

"How have you managed being single all this while, Iheoma?"

"Ada, I'm not single. I have my boy, Osita, and he's the sweetest five-year-old. I'm also seeing someone, you know?"

"What I mean is…"

"I know what you mean." Iheoma cut her off. "How have I managed being a single mother? I do just fine my dear. What has happened? Are you and Adrian breaking up?" Iheoma couldn't stop herself from asking.

"No, we are not. Something has just come up and I won't make the wedding. Can I call you back tomorrow?"

"Ada, something is wrong and I can sense it. You've never asked me about being single before and it's not like you to back away from what could be the biggest day in a friend's life. Let me tell you a bit about why I never married Osita's father. He didn't know what he wanted and he let his family and friends dictate his life. He may have loved me, but not enough to ask me to be his wife. He never knew I was pregnant when I left him and that was the whole point. I was not going to trap him with the baby, and because I knew being pregnant is not good enough reason to get married. I am responsible for my happiness, not some man. This your so-called family thing *sef*, I hope it's not about you and Adrian? I've always admired both of you, but sweetheart, the truth is, if it's not working and whatever damage is irreparable, be brave enough to walk away before it's too late. Life is too short."

"Thank you," Ada simply said. She understood the implications of the last statement, but with a child in the middle of things, walking away was not an easy choice.

"Is he seeing another woman? Or did he raise his hands to you?" Iheoma asked. She presumed that it was either one or the other, but she had to admit that the thought of Adrian being violent to anyone, not to mention Ada, was incomprehensible.

"Iheoma, I can't talk about this now. I will call you later and maybe then we can talk about it. Good night."

She hung up the phone and was again enveloped by the strange silence that had surrounded her ever since she let Adrian go. Ego was now having dinner in the dining room by the kitchen. The television was on with the volume turned down. Ada's invisible wall kept out thenoise, leaving her alone with her thoughts and worries.

Hard as she tried, she could not erase the image of herself and Adrian making love. He certainly had remained consistent with his approaches. But there had never been that many, not as many as she would have loved. In the first few months of their marriage, they made love at least three times a week, but this had quickly waned and now they managed it three times in a month. He had once confessed that he was not so into sex. She could not complain or argue since she had no prior experience. Yet she couldn't help but feel inadequate when her girlfriends joked about how they were getting it every night from their men. She joined in their fun, never admitting that her sex life was not as adventurous or even half as frequent as theirs. Then, some nights, Adrian was so passionate. She would melt as his hot lips enclosed on her nipples, slowly sucking and licking them. How did he pull it off? Was he physically in bed with her on those nights or was he imagining her as a man?

Life is too short! Iheoma had warned. Ada had to focus on what next, and that was having herself and her daughter examined. After that, she would start making plans for the future.

◉ ◉ ◉

LONG AFTER Adrian left Abdul's apartment, he was not sure he had found the answer he was searching for, or if he had new questions to contend with. One thing was certain though, Abdul was a happy soul. He was comfortable with his choice to come out to his family, and was now living a full and fulfilling life. Adrian wondered what it would have been like had he made the same choices. He feared to think of what kind of acceptance that would have greeted him. It was all about acceptance after all. It always had been for him.

When he thought about this he thought about *showers of love.* As a boy, at about seven or eight years old, he adored his father. When his father came out of the bathroom, he would move to the balcony to comb out his thick Afro with a wooden fork-like comb. Light drops of water still trapped in the hair would drizzle down. In his young mind, Adrian had believed these were showers of love so was always sure he sneak out to the balcony and sit directly underneath his father. This way he could be touched by his love. It was the closest he ever felt to his father. The ritual had become so important to him then, as he realised rather early that he was not the favourite of either of his parents. They loved him to some degree, he knew that much, but not like Chiedu who was his mother's favourite, or Chika who was his father's champion. Chiedu was the first son and was older than Adrian by five years. Chika was the last and exhibited a rare intelligence at his young age. He was younger than Adrian by only a year. Adrian was the middle child, who was always falling ill and was extremely shy as well.

Their mother treated Chiedu like a king. He never had to do any kind of house chores and was always shown off to her friends like the heir apparent. Chika enjoyed being lifted in the air and shrieked with glee as he pretended to be an airplane in his father's strong arms. He also followed their father to the recreational club and watched him play billiards. All Adrian could do was watch from his little corner with an uneasy smile on his face, not really wanting to be tossed up in the air like Chika because he was scared of heights, but wanting some kind of recognition and acceptance. When he was lucky, he got a smile but sometimes he wasn't even noticed. This was why his little showers of love were so important to him.

He smiled wryly thinking of those days, and wondered why his mind had gone there. It was so long ago and for years now he had forgotten that he had been that little sad boy. He wasn't even Adrian then. Everyone called him Ebele. His family still did, but he had fought for years to reinvent himself and erase any trace of Ebele.

It was dark when he got to Chiedu's house in Apapa. The gatekeeper let him drive in. He noticed Chika's car was also there. It had been a while since all three brothers were together in the same place. As he got out of his car, it struck him that maybe he had made a mistake by coming here. He certainly was not ready to face his family with the whole truth. He could see the lights in the living room through the voile drapes. The security lights shone from the top of the gatehouse illuminating the entire compound, and Adrian could hear the chirping sounds of locusts announcing their hidden presence.

As he got to the front porch, the door opened slowly and Chiedu's imposing build covered the doorframe. He wasn't smiling or frowning. His face was expressionless. How he looked like their father! Adrian thought. He was an exact copy of photographs of their father in his youth, but his head was as close to bald as possible, no Afro. Adrian had always been glad about this; seeing Chiedu in an Afro would have disturbed him. It would have been too much to contend with.

"Ebele..." Chiedu had a quiet drawl.

Only then did Adrian realize that they had been looking at each other for over a minute already. He muttered something inaudible as he walked up the stairs.

"Hi Chiedu!" He finally said. "It's almost as if you were expecting me."

Chiedu looked right at Adrian as he spoke. It was obvious that he was holding back from saying something. It dawned on Adrian then that his brother already knew.

"I see Chika is here as well." Adrian did not know what else to say to diffuse the lethal silence. "May I at least come in?"

Chiedu stepped aside. The house was quiet. Chiedu's two kids must have already been in bed, and his wife was nowhere in sight. Sitting in the living room with his head resting on his clasped hands was Chika. Momentarily, their eyes met. Adrian stepped into the living room and took a seat backing the dining area. The room was cold.

Chiedu remained standing in the middle of the room and after a while all three brothers felt the impact of their silence. Their unspoken words rang as loud as vocal confessions. It was as if they wished silence would make the issue simply go away so they would not have to confront it.

"Your kids are already in bed! What about Ese?" Ese was Chiedu's wife.

Chiedu reluctantly answered. "They are all fine."

"Good. What about you Chika? And Kathryn and your

boy, Nelson?"

"Fine…fine!"

The uncomfortable silence returned. Adrian remembered a night like this long before, when they were all kids. Their parents had gone out for a company dinner and the children were left alone with the housemaid. They had been playing hide-and-seek and after about three rounds they were bored. Chika then came up with the idea of rolling down the thirty-two-step cement staircase that led to the cellar. They found an old carton that must have once contained one of their electronic systems, and nominated Adrian to be folded inside and rolled down the stairs in the name of fun. Adrian was skeptical and worried.

"It looks dangerous," he whined. "Why can't you go instead?" He was looking at Chiedu.

He responded sternly. "Stop being such a sissy, Ebele. We are all having fun and nothing bad will happen."

"I don't like the dark and it's dark in the carton."

"Maybe I should go first?" Chika suggested.

"No!" Chiedu said harshly, his eyes boring wickedly at Chika. "Ebele will go first."

"I don't want to play this game…please!"

"Stop being a girl," Chiedu taunted back. He wrapped his arms round Adrian's skinny shoulders. "I promise I will let you play with me and my friends in school if you go first. I'm sure you will like that!"

Adrian nodded uneasily. He always wanted to play with Chiedu and his friends at school, but they laughed and made fun of him. This wasn't how they treated Chika. He would have particularly liked to play with Obinna, one of Chiedu's friends whom he had developed a strange fondness for. Whenever Obinna was around, Adrian's eyes lit up and he felt his heart flutter. When Obinna smiled at anything Adrian said, he was overjoyed for the rest of the day for being noticed.

And so he put on a brave face as he allowed his brothers to seal him up in the carton, catching briefly the look they both exchanged. He closed his eyes tightly at the first thrust of pain when his head and bones smashed against the cement of the stairs. Trapped, he screamed in pain and begged them to make it stop, but all he heard was the undisguised laughter of his brothers. He could still hear it faintly when he finally got to the bottom of the stairs,. His head was throbbing, his bones ached, but he was weeping only quietly so they would not hear him. Neither Chiedu nor Chika went down the stairs that night.

That incident happened ages ago, yet Adrian remembered it so clearly. He felt right back in familiar territory, with his brothers teaming up against him. He could feel their accusing eyes passing judgment on him. He had never been part of their team, and even as adults they were never on his side. Chiedu and Chika always agreed with each other while Adrian was always alone, in the dark... crying.

"When did you hear?"

"I got a call at work." Chika refused to look at him.

"It's all lies, isn't it?" Chiedu said, more to convince himself.

Adrian held his stare and noticed the pain in his eyes. He wondered what his brother was thinking and feeling at this moment.

"Chiedu, Chika, I have had this secret since I was a child and I wasn't sure how to tell you about what I was going through."

"What secret?" Chiedu demanded. "You got married! You have a child! What secret?"

"It's okay," Chika said, trying to make Chiedu stop shouting.

"I am gay, Chiedu," Adrian said, standing up to face him. "I've always been and I've always known. Yes, I'm married and I have a kid but take away who and what I am. I hate that you had to find out the way you did, but I never had the courage to tell either of you."

"Jesus Christ!" Chiedu muttered. "What will mum and dad say?"

Chiedu walked away from his brothers straight to the bar. He poured himself a drink and sighed loudly. Chika joined him, serving himself a drink as well. They both sat without speaking, pondering what they had just heard.

Adrian watched them for a while but did not join them. He knew he was not invited but did not care as much as he would have when he was a child. In fact he felt a certain calm after telling them. He could not as yet analyze their reaction, but sharing this intimate part of his life with his brothers made him feel better. He had been forced to carry the truth about himself alone for thirty six years. Suddenly he felt as if a huge weight had evaporated. This must be that inner peace that Abdul had alluded to.

"What about Ada?" Chika spoke from the bar. "Does she know?"

Adrian nodded.

"And what has she said?" Chiedu asked.

"She's the reason I'm here tonight. She's upset and asked me to leave the house. I thought I would spend the night here."

"You should have told us this, years ago," Chika said, "when we were younger...before you got married."

"Why did you even get married?" Chiedu asked.

That was a question Adrian had posed to himself every day of the six years he had been married. But he knew the answer. He did it because he had been afraid to even accept himself.

Another incident from his youth flashed through Adrian's mind. He must have been about fifteen. He was home alone; Chiedu had gone out to visit friends, Chika was with their father playing tennis, and their mum had stepped out to the market. There was nothing else for Adrian to do but watch a movie that happened to be on cable. He could not remember its name but recalled it was a romantic comedy with a hilarious gay character. In the middle of the movie, Chiedu came in with a couple of his friends. The noise they produced was overwhelming and they all gathered round the television looking amused.

"Isn't that guy a faggot?" Chiedu's face looked disgusted and his tone conveyed as much.

"I don't know," Adrian had answered. "It's just a comedy."

Chiedu had a skeptical look. He grabbed the remote control and browsed through a couple of channels, finally stopping at a game of football. His friends all sighed their approval and positioned themselves strategically on the sofa and available chairs.

Adrian felt his temper rise. This always happened to him. No one ever respected what he wanted to watch on television.

"I was watching that movie," Adrian whispered to Chiedu, practically pleading. "Why would you want to watch a movie about faggots?" Chiedu replied, his voice booming loudly. "This is a live Man United match we are watching and by the way we are the majority vote."

"I was watching the movie first!"

"Let's take a vote then! Who wants to watch the faggoty movie?"

No one raised their hands up. They all were laughing at Adrian, even Obinna who was there. Adrian turned away in shame and left the room. He had felt a connection with the gay character so his brother's attitude scared him. It was clear then that his brother did not approve of people like him and "faggot" was offensive to Adrian. He would hate it if his brother ever referred to him so disdainfully and with that word in particular.

There had been other similar incidents in the past that made Adrian realize that he could not disclose his sexuality to his brothers.

"Ebele," Chika said, bringing him back to the present, "if you have always known this, why then did you get married?"

"Ada is a wonderful person. I was in love with her… I thought marrying her was the right thing to do. I made up my mind to suppress my need to be with a man."

"You should have told us," Chika stressed.

"I wish I could then," Adrian said. "But you guys have always hated gays, you know you do…"

"Ebele, how can you say this?" Chiedu asked. "You know what the Bible says about homosexuals… God forbids it! The law says it's a felony for a man to practice sodomy."

"I know what the Bible says. And it's open to different interpretations. The law you speak about has been dictated by the society we live in…. Some societies state that if an unmarried woman has sex with a man and it's discovered, the woman should be stoned to death, and that is law. Please tell me, because the law says so, does that make it right?"

"Come on, Ebele," Chiedu said, "these are different things."

"How so?" Adrian challenged. "Sharia is law for the Muslims in this country and many others. Who are we to say that what their law dictates is wrong? And if it's right, does that make it okay? If our society was positive about homosexuality or silent on the issue, would being gay be acceptable to you then?"

"This is not about me, Ebele," Chiedu said. "It's about the fact that you are married and have a family of your own. It's about how you can live with yourself knowing what you are."

Chika interrupted. "That's a bit harsh, Chiedu."

"But it's true, isn't it? Have you thought about what this is going to do to your family?" Chiedu looked at both his brothers. "Our family? Mum and Dad? Are you currently seeing a...*man?*"

"If it makes you feel any better, I have been faithful to Ada from the moment we got married. There has been no one else."

"Then why didn't you just keep this whole issue to yourself? No one had to know. We could all have just continued the way we were."

"I didn't wake up this morning and decide to ruin everybody's life. Before today, I never knew I was going to disclose this to any of you, but I had no choice in the matter. An ex-colleague decided to get back at me and the only way he knew how was to do this."

There was that potent silence again. Even the ticking of the clock could be heard. The three brothers were lost in their thoughts.

"Were you ever going to tell any one of us?" Chika asked finally.

"I don't know," Adrian said after a short pause.

And this was the truth. He honestly did not know if he would have been brave enough to tell anyone in his family on his own. He had also bought into the heterosexual idea that he was not normal and should be ashamed of his orientation. But his sexuality was not a habit, like picking your nose in public or farting indiscriminately. He knew it was biological, somehow. He had always been this way.

"I don't understand. You've always had girlfriends in

the past. How come?"

"I had female friends," Adrian corrected. "I had to make up girlfriends so people wouldn't think I was weird."

"And your male friends, were they all your lovers?"

Adrian laughed. He had expected that.

"No, Chiedu. I'm not a saint. I've had my lovers…and sorry if that sounds distasteful to you, but it's the truth."

Adrian stood up. He had come here looking for shelter for the night, but he knew now that he could not stay. He wasn't being chased away, but his brothers needed to come to terms with the big revelation. They would have to deal with thirty six years' worth of secrets and deception. He apppreciated that it was not going to be easy for them, though whatever they had to contend with now was nothing compared with what he had suppressed all those years. And Chiedu was right in saying that it was all about him. It was his life and his family and his issues.

"I have to go."

"You said Ada asked you to leave," Chika said. "Where are you going to go?"

"I'll stay in a hotel tonight."

"You can stay here."

"Or you can come stay in my house," Chika offered too, "I have enough rooms."

"Thank you, but I can't accept. I just want to be alone tonight to think about what steps to take next."

He walked to his car alone. He had insisted that he didn't want them to worry about seeing him off. He waved to the gatekeeper and squeezed a hundred naira note in his palm as he drove off. He only drove for about five minutes before he parked his car at a curb. His heart was beating fiercely and his head was pounding. When he looked out of his car into the star-lit sky, he noticed the full moon and at that moment felt lost.

3

It was the longest night of her life. She didn't sleep at all. She just tossed and turned.

Ada had changed the bedspread. It still had the strong smell of Adrian's cologne. Any time she closed her eyes, she saw an endless stream of men, pretty men, and in their midst, her husband Adrian. She was hung up on the thought of Adrian in bed with another man. How many had there been? Was it possible that he may have been infected then infected her and their daughter? Did everyone else know about Adrian? Her friends? Did all *their* friends know?

She felt better now that she had switched her cell phone off and unhooked the landlines in the house. After the call from Iheoma she was not ready to speak with anyone else. She was afraid, too, that Adrian would have tried calling or worse still, one of his brothers. But still sleep refused to come. After about an hour, she stopped trying. Instead, she got on her knees and prayed. She prayed for many things, one being for morning to come soon. By 6.00 a.m. she gave up any hope of sleep. She switched on the television in the bedroom. This had always been part of her waking routine, to tune in to CNN so she could listen to the latest news while she prepared for the day. This morning she needed it all the more, needed the noise of the television to drown out the choking silence she had endured all through the night. She needed some kind of distraction.

Ada woke Isioma shortly after she got up, instructing her to prepare breakfast for Ego. When Isioma asked if she should first give Ego a bath, Ada informed her she would do it today. She went to Ego's room. Her daughter looked beautiful sleeping on her little bed. Ada stood for a long time just staring at her. Smiling fondly, Ada gently tapped Ego awake and lifted her in her arms while Ego protested sleepily. The girl wrapped her little arms round Ada's neck and held on tightly as she was carried to the bathroom. Ada filled the bathtub with warm water, undressed Ego, and soaked her in the tub. She washed her hair first and then gently sponged her clean. Ego had now woken up properly, and chatted about school and her teacher and her friends. Ada smiled with self-indulgence, not hearing anything but vaguely aware that her daughter had been speaking to her. She was doing everything mechanically. Functioning as if she had been programmed to do so. Wash, dry, cream up, dress.

"Mummy!" Ego said with confusion in her tiny voice. "This is not my uniform!"

Ada was holding up a pink-and-white-checkered pinafore dress. It was one of Ego's favourites. She loved wearing it to parties or to go out visiting with her parents.

"Yes, darling it's not your school uniform. You are not going to school today. We are going to visit the doctor."

Ego asked with worried lines on her brow; "Are we sick, mummy? I don't like the hospital. They give injections there."

Ada smiled and assured her that there would be no injections, that they would just have a routine check-up and there would be lots of ice cream afterwards. This delighted Ego. She was happy all morning and even ate up her breakfast. Her jovial mood put Ada at ease.

While Ego was still eating under the supervision of Isioma, Ada went up to her room to shower. She chose a simple two-piece batik dress, a gold chain with a crucifix and a gold watch. She used light make-up and was happy at her reflection in the mirror. There was the need to keep up appearances, after all.

Only after dressing did she switch on her phones. She had five voice messages from Chika, Adrian's brother, and also a text asking her to please call back. She knew what he wanted to talk about, though he had not left any clues. She would call him later.

She placed a call to her assistant, Angela, to inform her that she would not be in the office that morning. She also instructed her not to disturb her with any calls, except if there was a real emergency involving one of her top clients. It was at moments like these that Ada felt relieved to be running her own business. She dictated her time. She had a booming interior design and decorating outfit, and her clientele included wives of senators and other politicians, as well as some well-known local celebrities. Her business and her success would not have happened if Adrian had not pushed her, believed in her and invested a whole lot of capital to jump-start the business.

The thought of Adrian brought a wave of bitter anger in her. He had not even called to leave a message as his brother did. Closing her eyes, she willed herself to keep calm. There would be no point letting Ego and Isioma see her disturbed, or giving any sign to the doctor and nurses that all was not well at home.

Ada didn't have any breakfast herself. She instructed Isioma to use the dry fish in the freezer with the vegetable that was bought the day before to make stew, and boil some slices of yam for lunch. When she was sure Isioma understood what she would have to do once she returned from school later in the afternoon, Ada got into her car with Ego and headed for the hospital.

She was among the first patients there and in no time was speaking with her doctor. Smiling nervously, she informed him that she would like to be tested, along with her daughter, for any STDs. She gave no excuse and her stern look dared the doctor to ask why. He didn't, and instead informed her professionally that it was now quite easy to get tested, including for HIV and AIDS. Though there was still a wait to get the results, it would not take days as it used to. Ada took all this in quietly.

In less than an hour the tests had been completed. When asked if she would rather return for the results in a couple of hours or the next day, Ada opted to wait instead. Her doctor politely hinted that she should go; he ran a busy practice and very soon other patients would crowd the waiting area and, in that atmosphere, nothing would remain private. Everyone was interested in the next person's business. Ada got the message.

"As soon as the results are out I can call you instead," the doctor promised.

Ada nodded her appreciation and left with Ego. She was scared and confused. What if the results were positive? Would she ever be able to forgive Adrian, or herself?

She took Ego to a nice little ice cream place that had a playpen for young children. Ego was more than happy to have a large scoop of strawberry ice cream and run off to join the other two kids playing in the colorful rubber castle. Ada watched her to make sure she got along with the other kids before she let her mind wander off.

It was the third year into their marriage, shortly after the birth of Ego. She noticed her sex life with Adrian had waned considerably. She took it as nothing initially, but then he began to work longer hours. He even started going to work on Saturdays. He stopped making moves on her, and she didn't know how to tell him that she needed him to be intimate sometimes. She believed it was the man's role to initiate sex, not the woman's. She worried then that he would have thought her common if she took the initiative. Now, she wondered if all that time he was sneaking off to see another man. Those late nights he spent at the office. The Saturdays away from home! Could it be?

She had eventually found a way to let him know she wanted to be touched like a woman. One night she stayed awake in bed waiting for him. He came back from the office just after 9.00 p.m. and when he finally got into bed, over thirty minutes later, she started sobbing quietly but audibly enough for him to hear. He finally turned round to ask her what the problem was. And she told him.

"Do I repulse you, Adrian?"

"No, why would you think that?"

"Then why won't you touch me? Am I ugly? Why don't you find me sexual anymore?"

"No, no, no…" Adrian kissed her tear-filled eyes. "I think…no, I believe you are the most beautiful woman I would ever have."

They made love that night and several times each night for the rest of the week. Ada's happiness was short-lived though, as Adrian's interest faded again after about a month. This time she did not push or even try to cajole him into making love with her. She just had to accept her man the way he was. He was simply not interested in sex. That's the way he was. Instead, she decided to build a career and focus on her business. Adrian had been more than happy to support her in this venture. She suspected his enthusiasm was fuelled by the hope that she would not demand more of him emotionally or sexually.

Her cell phone startled her back from her emotional

journey into the past. The beating in her heart was fast, hard
and threatening to tear out from her chest. The results were
out! This must be the doctor calling to let her know. She
looked momentarily at Ego before she picked up her phone.
But she recognized the number as Chika's and sighed in
soft relief.

"Ada, how are you? I've been trying to reach you all
through last night. Are you okay?"

She had to lie.

"Where are you? I called your office and Angela said
you were not coming in today."

"I had something to do, Chika."

"I have to see you. About Ebele… Adrian."

Ada was quiet. She didn't know how to respond to
that. She wished she had more time to think through her
next steps, to compose herself and be strong in front of the
world.

"Ada, are you still there?" Chika's voice boomed out of
her tiny phone.

"Yes… Come by the house this afternoon." Why she
said that, she did not know. The words just forced their way
out of her mouth before she could stop herself.

"OK, I will." Chika too had sensed the doubt in her
voice. "Are you sure you are all right? How is Ego?"

"Fine, we are fine Chika. I will speak with you later.
Bye Chika and thanks for calling."

She quickly ended the call before Chika could ask
any more questions. No sooner had she hung up than her
phone rang out again. Without looking at the number, she
answered irritably.

"Chika," she began, "I understand your concern, but
I'm okay and…"

"Ada," a calm professional voice said, "Doctor Charles
here with the results."

"Charles!" Ada said breathlessly. "That was quick."

"I told you the process is faster than most people believe," he said. "Good news, you are both clean."

"Thank God!" Ada whispered a silent prayer of relief.

"But…" Charles was saying.

"Oh my God!" Ada cried. "You just said everything was okay!"

"Nothing serious, Ada," Charles assured her. He was still surprised by her businesslike attitude that morning. "Ego has symptoms of malaria. I will drop some medicine off for her on my way home from work if that's okay."

"Thank you, Charles," Ada muttered in relief. "You don't have to bother. I can be in the clinic in the next fifteen minutes."

"Ada, I know it's none of my business, but your sudden paranoia about having an HIV test is worrying. I hope your husband will be having himself tested as well?"

"Thank you, Charles," Ada said tightly before she hung up. He may be her doctor and friend, but he was not her confidant nor did he have a right to pry into her private life.

One thing stuck in her mind though: they were clean. They were okay and disease-free. Oh thank God! She felt lighter. She felt a glimmer of hope.

◙ ◙ ◙

ADRIAN SPENT the night at Kuramo Lodge. He loved the cozy intimacy the hotel provided. The rooms were small but very comfortable and tastefully furnished, just like so many similar three-star hotel rooms in other parts of the world he had visited. But enjoying the hotel's ambience was the last thing on his mind. His troubled mind had kept his eyes wide open for the duration of the night.

He had showered and hoped that his already tired body

and equally worn-out soul would succumb to the inviting warmth of the soft bed. But after futile tossing and turning, he resigned himself to no sleep.

His mind roamed everywhere imaginable. He thought about Ada and what would be going through her mind. He thought of his beautiful daughter. He thought about his encounter with his brothers. But mostly his mind kept going way back to his childhood, as if whatever answers he was looking for were somehow hidden in those suppressed memories.

At eight o'clock in the morning he checked out of his room and gave a generous tip to the friendly concierge. He had to get home and change for work. Work! The thought of work and the office seemed so strange and foreign. The office had served as his safe haven. It was a place he could lose himself in, and not focus on his weakness. He had let himself become the ultimate professional, the stereotypical workaholic.

Even though he wasn't expecting to meet Ada at home, he was nonetheless nervous that she just might be there when he opened the door. The house was empty. He had never experienced such total and sheer emptiness before in his life. The emptiness in his heart was crushing. Nothing in his home was recognizable to him. The living room in its curtained darkness gave out an unwelcoming gloom. Gone was the laughter of his daughter and sparkle of his wife. Something struck him then; he had never really been a part of any of that, only a passive observer. He had never really been part of this family. He may have been the husband who escorted his beautiful wife to parties and other social functions; the father who doted on his lovely child and showed her off when friends came over; the dependable family man who provided. Yet he had been all these things without actually being there. He had simply gone through the motions in robotic mode, not really thinking or feeling. He smiled when he had to smile, played when he had to play, and he had become good at it. He had even fooled himself into believing that he was finally like other normal heterosexual men.

He took a quick shower, selected a black single-breasted suit, light blue shirt and matching tie, and only spent a second staring at his reflection in the mirror before leaving the room. He was quick to notice that the picture of himself and Ada by the dresser had been turned face down. This gave him a pinch of pain in his heart. He rushed out of the house wanting to be far away from its gloom, yet knowing he was responsible for it.

The imposing signage at the top of the multiplex announcing 'DialPlus' in its brand colours of red and blue no longer impressed. Adrian had hoped that getting to the office would help him focus on other things, but he knew it was not the same place for him anymore. He used to be so proud of his achievements here. DialPlus was now the nation's number one mobile telecommunications company with branches nationwide.

Adrian remembered nine years earlier when he first heard that the well-known American billionaire entrepreneur, Wilbur Lander, would be launching DialPlus America in Nigeria's telecommunications market. There had been so much excitement and speculation in the news, and industry insiders knew what this meant for the already existing mobile telecommunications companies. Adrian had seen a huge opportunity and quickly applied for a marketing position in the business development unit, which he got easily. After two years of hard work and high profile networking, he was transferred to be a team leader in the human development unit of the company; everyone agreed he had excellent people skills as well as leadership qualities. Today, he was the head of the business risk unit and his friends would fondly call him the 'SSS' for the headman in charge, the CEO.

He had made some enemies on his climb to the top, which could not be helped. Adrian understood that not everyone was happy to see other people grow or progress in life. This was very much a Nigerian thing. He remembered his mother advising all her children to make sure to acquire 'native sense' and not just learn Western, naïve 'civility.' She would always say, "…remember that not everyone who smiles with you loves you." And this was so true with Tayo Onasanya. He had started off as a friend of Adrian's, as they had both worked in the same place before switching over to DialPlus. Adrian signed his contract first and had a good head-start on the job before Tayo joined, a fact that Tayo secretly loathed. But they got along seemingly well until Adrian's first promotion. Tayo's attitude changed after this. Adrian discovered much later that Tayo too had been coveting that position. It got worse over the years as it seemed that every major position that Tayo lobbied for, Adrian or someone he recommended got. On the surface Tayo was always smiling at Adrian and even saying, for the benefit of listening ears, that they were the best of friends, but Adrian had not been fooled. He knew Tayo did not like him much anymore and, given an opportunity, would stab him in the back. But the truth was that Adrian was not threatened by Tayo or even bothered. As far as he was concerned the only element that connected them to any degree was work. They were not friends

Only once had Tayo come close to being a real threat to Adrian and that was as a result of a business trip they took together three years earlier to Johannesburg. Their business contact there, Judith Keppel, was an old friend of Adrian who knew he was gay, and had mistakenly blurted it out to

Tayo over a private lunch once. On their flight back to Lagos, Tayo whispered to Adrian on the plane, "don't worry, your secret is safe with me. Judith told me." Adrian was horrified but had chosen to ignore him and pretend he hadn't heard a thing. For weeks and months Adrian worried about word getting out in the office. But no one said anything, no gossip, and no fingers, and after six months he relaxed. Tayo had told no one, but still, those mornings when they crossed paths, Tayo would lock eyes with him and give him a knowing smile shadowed with a discreet wink.

Today as Adrian walked into the office, people were stealing glances at him. There were muted whispers and even discreetly pointing fingers. The only difference was that Tayo was no longer there. But his damaging presence could be felt. After mumbling a few good mornings Adrian shuffled into his office and locked the door behind him. Resting his head on the door, he closed his eyes and sighed. His office was located on the third floor of the complex, at the far end of the building from the elevator. It was the biggest office on that floor and normally took two minutes to cross from the elevator to his office. This morning, it had felt more like two hours.

So they knew! It was a realization Adrian would have to accept and deal with. Given his senior position, he doubted that many people would have the guts to question him about his sexuality, but he did not want the shame of them thinking that he was queer and obscene. Abdul had said the night before that it seemed Adrian was ashamed of his past; what Abdul actually wanted to say was that he was ashamed of his sexuality. He had been for years. He had wanted it to be his little secret. He had even hoped that he would wake up one morning and find himself cured, straight.

Adrian had ten voice messages and at least fifty unread emails waiting for him. Two of the messages were from the commercial director, John Coker, who was his immediate boss. They were asking him to call him as soon as he got in, and sounded both tense and urgent. The majority of the emails concerned the termination of five staff members, including Tayo Onasanya, for misappropriation and illegal diversion of funds to private accounts. Adrian made a mental note to forward all completed paperwork and findings to the board of directors.

"May I come in, sir?" A dark-skinned, handsome man poked his head into Adrian's office. He was dressed smartly but casually in a long-sleeved shirt, without a tie, tucked into a pair of snug trousers. Adrian looked up at him. Rotimi. He was one of Adrian's prodigies. An intelligent and ambitious young man full of promise and potential. Adrian had picked him up years earlier when they first met, and made sure he got a temp job as office assistant. Now Rotimi was a call centre agent fulltime, and had also bagged a diploma in between his work.

Adrian knew Rotimi saw him as a big-brother figure and mentor. In fact Rotimi was so protective of Adrian that he would get into a fist fight to defend his name and integrity. Unfortunately, he listened too much to office gossip and negative talk and always ran back to keep Adrian informed on what people were saying about him. Most times, Rotimi was afraid that Adrian might be the victim of some office politics or power play. Adrian always assured him at all times that he was okay and had nothing to be afraid of.

"Rotimi, yes, come in."

Rotimi entered the office and shut the door behind him. Adrian motioned for him to take a seat, which he accepted. He looked tired and worried.

"How are you sir?" Rotimi asked in an attempt to sound jovial.

"Fine, Rotimi and thanks for asking," Adrian said as he

interlocked his fingers while resting his elbows on his desk.

"Sir, this fraud thing has got many people talking and speculating all kinds of rubbish."

"I can only imagine," Adrian said smiling. "People will always talk, Rotimi, and I have told you this several times. Don't let this bother you."

Rotimi shook his head in rejection.

"This time it's different, sir."

"How so?" Adrian was afraid to know the answer to the question.

Rotimi hesitated for a minute or so. He avoided direct eye contact with Adrian and wrung his sweaty palms together in a nervous play.

"Yes?"

"Well sir, some people are saying you set Mr. Tayo up."

"That is ludicrous. I did not set him up and I certainly did not start an investigation on him. The internal audit unit from the U.S. instigated the investigation. I was only drawn in after evidence had been gathered and submitted to my department to verify."

Adrian felt the need to explain this to Rotimi. He needed someone else, other than those in the know, to appreciate the real truth behind the investigation. He too had heard the rumour about his being hell bent on getting rid of some staff.

"I tried telling them that you had nothing to do with it. But they believe that you singled out the Yoruba people you felt threatened by and made sure you got them sacked, especially Mr. Tayo."

Adrian understood the tribal undertone of the case. The only people affected had been Yoruba. Over the years some Ibo staff members, Adrian inclusive, had been fortunate to be recognized for their hard work and promoted to high-ranking and strategic positions within the company. Some of these promotions had been possible owing to Adrian's recommendations. But what many were apt to forget was that Adrian had recommended as many Yoruba people as he had Ibos. The Hausas had a firm hold on the top corporate positions in DialPlus offices in the north, with the exception of the Abuja office, which was run by a Yoruba man. But Adrian was totally weary of such office politics that he never paid much attention.

"Not only that," Rotimi added quietly, "but they are also saying it was because Mr. Tayo had something on you."

"Now that is stupid," Adrian said. "I think you need to get back to your desk, you have work to do. There's nothing to any of that."

"They are saying that you are *gay* and Mr. Tayo knew about you and so you decided to get rid of him. Is this true?"

Before Adrian could determine what question Rotimi wanted an answer to, whether he was gay or whether there was any truth to his getting rid of Tayo because of this, his desk phone rang.

"Good morning, Adrian speaking." After a pause he said, "Good morning John, yes I'll drop by your office immediately." He hung up shortly afterwards.

"Thank you for coming over, Rotimi. Please return to your desk and I will see you later."

Adrian stood up indicating to Rotimi that the meeting was indeed over. There was some doubt in Rotimi's face as he got up and headed for the door. He took one last unsure look at Adrian before opening the door and walking out of the office.

◎ ◎ ◎

AS SOON as Adrian stepped into John's office, it was obvious why he had been called. The news had got to John too. Though John acted as pleasantly as always, Adrian could detect an uneasiness in his normally cool countenance. He offered Adrian a seat but quickly withdrew his hand after a brief handshake. It was as if John was afraid that by touching him he would be infected.

"Thanks for coming in," John said as soon as they were both seated, "and thank you for the thorough work you put into the fraud case."

"I really did nothing John," Adrian replied with ease. "You should be thanking the internal auditors, not me. All I did was to verify information passed on to my department."

The response was a little absent-minded. "Yes, yes… I'm just surprised about the people involved… Tayo and the others."

Adrian remained quiet. He knew it would be unwise to voice any opinion at this point. John may be his superior, but he had a history of getting sensitive information from people and then using it against them later, when the need arose. Another thing was that John liked Tayo. Adrian had to be careful; he would have to apply some native sense.

"Is there something you would like to tell me, Adrian?" John asked. "I've heard some things."

"Everything I have to say was presented to the board yesterday. I believe I covered all areas of my findings."

John looked at him and shrugged. Adrian knew exactly what he wanted to know, but was not going to play ball.

"OK then. Please forward the report to me by email as soon as you get back to your office."

"I will do that, John. Will that be all for now?"

"Yes, Adrian. Thank you for coming."

As Adrian shut the door behind him, he felt a cold chill run down his spine and broke out in a cold sweat. How much more of this could he live through?

◎ ◎ ◎

ADA SPENT the morning and afternoon driving around
the island, avoiding any spot where friends or professional
acquaintances might recognize her. She screened all her
calls and only answered two from her office, which turned
out to be important. Iheoma had also phoned, but she did
not answer. She was not ready for her yet. Ada ended up
spending the whole morning in the same ice-cream place.
They had a wonderful menu, and she ordered lunch of fried
rice and chicken for herself and her daughter.

Chika was already waiting for her by the time she got
home that afternoon. She had stopped first at the hospital
to pick up the prescription for Ego and the results of the
tests, and then dropped Ego off at Amaka's house for piano
lessons.

Isioma was back from school and had let Chika in.
When Ada saw him, legs crossed on the sofa, watching
television, she was struck by how alike the brothers were.
One could easily mistake Chika for being older than Adrian,
but the face and jawline were unmistakable. Ada had always
gotten along better with Chiedu for his fun-loving attitude
and their shared love for the same football team. He had
been in London during the last English Premiership and
she would call him often to discuss it. The phone bill had
made Adrian so furious. Chika, on the other hand, was on
the reserved side. He was always nice to her but not overly
so. There seemed to be an invisible boundary between him
and Ada, and Ada always found herself trying to play the
perfect in-law whenever he was around.

"Ada," Chika said, standing up as soon as he noticed
her, "how are you?"

"I'm fine, Chika. I hope you haven't been waiting for
too long?"

She walked into the living room and gestured for Chika to take his seat as she lowered herself on one of the chairs. She placed her purse and the envelopes containing the test result by the side of the seat, between her body and the cushion, so that Chika could not spy what it was she was carrying.

"I just got here. What about Ego?"

"Today is Friday, she's having piano lessons. May I offer you a drink?"

"No thank you, I'm OK."

Silence, again. Neither of them wanted to bring up the real subject, but it was certainly clear what they were thinking. Ada's eyes trailed away to the television where she made out images of US troops in a demolished village square in Iraq. There was an overturned, burning vehicle with a UN sticker on its side. As the television camera panned to a stack of burning dead bodies, Ada shifted her eyes away and sighed deeply.

"What do you intend to do with this situation with Adrian?"

"I don't know." Ada's reply was truthful and caused tears to well up in her eyes and run down her cheeks in a slow but steady flow. She cursed herself inwardly. She was supposed to be strong in front of him. She had thought she had shed her last tears the night before!

"I'm so sorry," Chika said as he passed his handkerchief to her, but she declined and used the back of her hands to wipe off the tears.

"I didn't mean to cry. It's just so hard to understand all this."

"I know. But one thing is for sure, and that's Adrian loves both you and Ego."

Ada eyed him dubiously. She didn't mean to, but couldn't stop herself. Right now she didn't need to hear about how much Adrian loved her. He had deceived her all these years and she was not sure what to believe about him anymore.

"We saw him last night, Chiedu and I. And he was totally crushed. All he could talk about was how he hurt you. I don't think he ever meant to, Ada."

"How can you say for sure? Did you know? Have you always known that he was gay?"

Chika hesitated for a second before responding.

"No, I never knew…or suspected."

"So you don't know for sure whether he meant to hurt me or not," Ada added icily.

"Adrian is not like that, Ada. And you know it. This is something beyond our control or imagination."

"What are you saying?" Ada cried. "You have no idea what I have to go through. I have to come to terms with having to explain all this to our daughter one day. I have to deal with having to explain to my family why we are separated if we decide to split, and I have to face our friends. What if this gets out? I have to deal with it every day for the rest of my life."

"We are family and we will deal with whatever issues together as a family," Chika said comfortingly.

"Do you know what I had to do today?" Ada asked. "I went for an HIV/AIDS test today with Ego."

Her words stung the air and Chika felt an uneasiness wash over him as he contemplated the result. His thoughts were suspended for that moment. He knew she could see the worry lines that now marked his face.

"And…"

"It was negative, thank God!" Ada sighed. "But it could have been different. We could have been infected and only God knows what would have happened then… Do you even have an idea of what I felt as I waited for the results? You can't imagine all the things that went through my head."

"Thank God!" Chika whispered a silent prayer. "Adrian says he hasn't been with any man ever since you came along."

"So I guess that makes it better!" Ada retorted sarcastically. "So Chika, tell me what you will have me do in my situation. Should I continue to live like this? Should I just pretend that everything is okay?"

No answer.

"Last night I stayed awake all night thinking about my life," Ada went on. "I was asking myself all through if it was my fault. Maybe I turned him away. Maybe I wasn't doing something right... You can't know how inadequate I felt."

"I agree, Ada," Chika concurred. "But I believe he has changed. He wants to be with you."

"He told you this? Chika can you tell me how I can ever erase the image of Adrian and another man having sex from my head?"

Ada could see and sense how uncomfortable Chika was feeling. It was good for him. He could not just breeze in here and tell her things were going to be okay, that Adrian loved her. Sharing her pain made her feel better. It was nice to know that she was not the only one suffering this. It made the burden less. But this was not enough for her.

"Or maybe you can tell me how to behave in such a situation."

"I don't have answers for you."

"I thought as much."

Later on that night after Chika had gone and Ego had gone to bed, Ada was alone once again battling with her thoughts.

◻ ◻ ◻

ADRIAN WAS no stranger to blocking out issues from his mind. He had been denying his sexuality for many years and had almost become an expert at it. It was easy. All he had to do was focus on work. By channelling all his energy into work, he wouldn't have to think about anything else. He had to block out the pain; block out the fear. And he did just that.

The paperwork for the fraud case took him about two hours to finish satisfactorily. He had no fewer than twenty emails to respond to, which he did. Another hour and a half went into that. He had other reports and cases to work on, which he had left for far too long. His phone never stopped ringing and he spent some time answering the important calls and returning some others. He felt totally energized and all worries were locked up in a distant place until Nkechi barged into his office. Despite the shock, Adrian masked his nervousness with a crooked smile.

"Addy," Nkechi cooed out his nickname in her endearing fashion, "I know you are busy, but we have to talk."

"Nkky, can't we do it another time? I'm swamped with work, you know."

"Don't be silly." Nkechi entered and shut the door behind her. "You must always have time for your in-law, Addy."

Adrian had always been captivated by Nkechi's confidence and forwardness. She was a short woman – five feet two inches. But her size was hardly noticed because of her larger-than-life personality. She had a very beautiful face, but that was not all. She also always made sure that her voice was heard. She was very opinionated, with the sharpest wit Adrian had ever encountered. When she stepped into a room, she owned it. She could not be ignored with her powerful dressing and excellent command of the English language.

As Nkechi sat down to face Adrian, gone was the jovial look. She now wore a serious, hard mien, but her worry was evident.

"Addy, the office atmosphere is lethal today," she began. "Everyone is scared that they may be under investigation… And they blame you. Poor you!"

"I'm trying not to think about it."

Nkechi stopped and focused her eyes on Adrian. Resting her right hand on his desk, she placed her index finger on her right cheek and tried to catch his eyes. Adrian did everything to avoid looking at her. He suddenly found himself rearranging files, opening and closing drawers, anything to keep him looking busy.

Nkechi at last continued, "Adrian…and there's the other stuff people are saying about…you."

Adrian didn't respond to this, afraid that any squeak from him would prompt Nkechi to pry further into his private life. It was bad enough that they were in-laws.

"Aren't you curious to know what everyone is saying?"

"I'm not responsible for those guys being fired," Adrian said defensively, "I didn't make them commit fraud."

"That's not what I meant," Nkechi said. "It's the other things they are saying."

Silence.

"Of course, I don't believe any of the rubbish people are saying," Nkechi said. "But I want to be able to look any one of them in the face and tell them to go to hell. So tell me, are you gay?"

Silence.

"*Adrian*…" Nkechi searched him for an answer. The moment their eyes locked, she knew. "Oh, my God!"

The realization of what Adrian wasn't saying, and what it meant, hit Nkechi hard. All she could think of was her cousin, Ada. She was responsible for their meeting and had encouraged their relationship until they got married.

"Adrian, how can you be gay? But you are married…to my cousin… You have a child."

"Nkechi, please let's not do this here," Adrian finally croaked. "I've not been gay since I got married. I love Ada, okay?"

"Oh my God! I have to call Ada… Does she know?"

"Yes, she does," Adrian admitted.

"And…? What did she say? What did she do?"

"She's not very happy. But I'm sure we will work things out."

"Oh God, no!" Nkechi screamed as she stood up. "Why didn't you tell me before?"

"I just couldn't."

Nkechi paced round the office trying hard to absorb Adrian's words. She was worried and kept muttering to herself as she moved from one corner of the room to the other. Whenever her eyes rested on Adrian, she shuddered and shook her head in disbelief. She had always respected Adrian and admired his steadfast professionalism, honesty and candour. But right now, this man in front of her was an absolute stranger, a stranger capable of the most convincing deception, a stranger who was married to her cousin.

"I have to go, Adrian. I have to call Ada."

As Nkechi rushed out of the office, Adrian experienced a crushing, suffocating feeling in his chest. The strong disapproval he had sensed from Nkechi was like a dagger stabbing at his conscience. He knew he had been judged and found guilty. She could not possibly understand what he was going through, nor appreciate the sacrifices he made for countless years. How was she to ever know that if she hadn't made such a fuss about his meeting Ada, and then facilitating their engagement, he wouldn't have been in the situation he was in right now? The truth was that before he met Ada, he had gone through some rather unfulfilling and disappointing relationships with men. At that point in his life, he had decided to be celibate and forget about emotional happiness. He knew he could achieve that. He had done it before. After one particular painful break-up with a lover, he had shut the door to relationships for a year and a half.

Nkechi's persistent plea for him to meet her cousin had set the ball rolling for a series of events that would lead to his marriage to Ada. Could he have stopped it earlier? Could he have just walked away and kept to his pact with himself? These questions he had asked himself countless times, and even now he did not know the true answers. But one thing remained valid to him: if he had not met Ada, he would never have married.

Adrian sighed. Was he just telling himself this to justify why he got married? Was he still afraid of confronting the truth? What indeed was the truth? The answer was a whisper in his ears – he had wanted to be accepted as a normal person. He wanted to fit in and not have people whispering about him behind his back, making assumptions. He also didn't want to be pitied by anyone. He had had his fill of rejection as a child, and of not being the perfect son or brother as expected of him.

God! Now he had more or less confirmed to Nkechi that he was gay. Apart from his silence, he had not even tried to deny his sexuality. He could have simply calmed her and denied all the talk with one of his charming smiles. But he didn't. It was that simple; he didn't want to. Not anymore. A part of him wanted her to know. After disclosing his sexuality to his brothers, Adrian was beginning to believe that as soon as he revealed himself to those close to him and got some kind of acceptance, the healing process for him would begin. After all, *what's the worst that can happen?* Abdul had said.

Every fibre in his body was screaming out for him to call Ada. He missed her warmth and the softness of his daughter's skin. He may not have been so involved with their lives but not having the security of their presence was killing him. He felt so naked and lonely. Though he had been a loner all his life he had never felt lonely.

He was so lonely now.

◎ ◎ ◎

WHEN NKECHI'S call came, Ada had guessed that it would be her. It was almost as if she had willed her to call. She wanted so much to talk to somebody from her family, but not just anyone, someone she could open up completely to, and just then the phone rang.

"Ada dear, how are you?" Nkechi's voice dripped with concern. "Oh my God, I only just heard."

"I'm fine, Nkechi. I don't understand what is happening... I got this call yesterday from a man who told me my Adrian is...is..."

"You don't have to say it," Nkechi said in a low voice. "I just confronted Adrian and he did not deny it either."

"I don't understand all this. Nkechi, what is happening to my family? What is wrong with Adrian?"

"I never knew, Ada! I wouldn't have let this happen."

Ada hardly heard what Nkechi had said and it suddenly occurred to her that she was whispering for some reason.

"Why are you whispering?"

There was a pause before Nkechi answered. "I'm placing this call from one of the stalls in the ladies' room. There's no private place in this damn office and walls have ears. It's bad enough that everyone is talking about Adrian, and being one of his supporters, I don't want to have to confirm it to them."

"How come you never suspected?"

Nkechi confessed. "He was always so quiet at work and so immaculately turned out and so polite that I mistook it for just polish."

"I had to go for an HIV test today."

Ada heard Nkechi's gasp from the other end of the phone. There was an intense silence, which was broken only when Ada spoke again.

"Both Ego and I tested negative, thank God!"

"Thank God!" Nkechi echoed. "I never even thought about that. After work, I will come over to see you, okay?"

"I'm okay, Nkechi. You can come to visit during the weekend. If you don't go home now, your husband will call for you wanting an explanation."

"I will call him now and tell him I will be with you," Nkechi insisted.

"No. What if he wants to know why?"

"Ada, you need someone there with you."

"You can't tell him," Ada said with urgency in her tone. "You can't tell anybody. Nobody in the family must know."

"They will find out eventually, Ada."

"I've not made up my mind on what to do. I can't have the family clouding my judgment before then."

"Do you still love him? I would understand if you do. The Adrian I know possesses great qualities that would be hard not to love. But who would have guessed…?"

"I don't know what I feel for him any more."

This was true. Reflecting hours later over the conversation with Nkechi, the question still hung over Ada, taunting her almost. Did she still love him? Could things still work out for both of them? What if she blinded her heart to the truth of his sexuality and made him promise to always remain faithful to her? Who would know the better?

She would, and the suspicion would always be there.

Ada was determined that no one in her family should find out about this yet. She needed to know for sure what she wanted to do. Getting family involved now would only complicate issues for her. She couldn't face the drama, the pity and the secret triumph of jealous relatives.

4

When he got Ada's call, Adrian's heart stopped beating. He thought he was going to suffocate. She sounded curt and distant but Adrian didn't care. He missed her.

"I've missed you, Ada," he said, not listening to what she was saying to him.

"Did you hear anything I just said?" Ada asked coldly. "Ego has been asking for you. She's been crying since yesterday…I don't know what to do,"

Just then, Adrian made out his daughter's muffled cry in the background. She was crying for him and his heart broke all over again. He truly missed them.

"Put her on the phone, Ada. Let me speak with her,"

He heard it all as she took in a deep breath and then said soothingly to their daughter that 'daddy' was on the phone.

"Daddy!" the tiny, teary voice said with a sniffle.

"Baby, how is my big girl?" Adrian cooed into the receiver.

"Daddy, where are you?" Ego asked as her sobbing slowly abated. "Mummy said you travelled but you didn't kiss me goodbye,"

"Sweetheart I kissed you while you slept," Adrian lied.

"When are you coming home?"

"I'm coming home soon, darling," Adrian replied, his

voice almost giving way to tears. "Daddy is coming home soon…give mummy the phone, okay?"

"Goodbye daddy…"

The finality of her parting words stung Adrian. When Ada came back on line, Adrian felt like screaming.

"I'm coming over, Ada. I have to see Ego."

"I don't think that's a good idea, Adrian," Ada said defiantly. "I don't know if I can handle seeing you right now."

"This is not about you, Ada. Our daughter wants to see her father. You are not the only one who is affected by this."

There was a silence. Adrian could hear Ada's restrained breathing, masking her seething anger over the phone line. He could also feel anger rising within him. She had no right to cut him off from his home, his family, no matter what. They would have to come together sooner or later to confront this issue.

"Ada," he continued with some restraint, "I'm coming over this afternoon to see both of you. It has been two days already."

It had been two days of torture for Adrian. He had continued to stay at the hotel, but knew he could not keep up with the expenses involved anymore and the loneliness was crushing him. He had blocked himself from the outside world in that time. It was enough having to deal with the uncomfortable atmosphere at the office. After work, when he got into his hotel room, he would switch off his cell phone and lock himself in.

"Okay," Ada said in resignation. "You can come over. But I don't know…"

"Thank you. I'll be there before one."

Adrian was almost euphoric as he prepared for his meeting with Ada and Ego. He even allowed himself to imagine that when he got there Ada would rush up to him and embrace him, planting feathery kisses on his cheeks and lips and proclaiming how much she loved him no matter what he was and what he had done in the past. He imagined Ego holding on to him and telling him that he was the best father in the whole world and, no matter what anyone would say, he would always remain her hero. In a perfect world, maybe this would be possible but coming down to reality he knew it would never be so, especially if the tone of Ada's voice was an indication of what to expect.

Adrian marvelled at how he had not let himself look further into the future to see where all this would lead to. He had been focusing on the here and now, trying to devise ways to survive every day. He was slowly trying to find acceptance of who he was and hope that the people that meant the most to him would also find acceptance somewhere within their hearts. At this stage, he needed their understanding and love, or he would lose faith in himself as well.

His car had gathered a thin coat of dust. He hadn't washed it in two days and it only now occurred to him that the security men at the office used to do it for him without any prompting, but since the issue with Tayo Onasanya, none had bothered. In fact, they no longer hung around to greet him in the morning or after work, when he usually squeezed the customary hundred naira bill into their expecting palms. Adrian made a mental note to take his car to the wash before he got to his home.

He replayed his last day at work that week and pondered on how dynamics in the office had changed as well. He had always been an early bird and most times he was the first person in the office. When the other staff started trickling in, anytime from 7.00 a.m., a number would come to his office to say hello and some even hung around long enough to enjoy a small chat and discuss their careers. He loved these little visits. He enjoyed inspiring people and usually was amazed by the quality of advice he gave out. He had once joked that if he were in the United States, he would have made a rather successful therapist. But the last two days had been very different. His office had been devoid of visitors. After his encounter with Nkechi, she had not come again to see him and had not answered his calls either. The only person who had been brave enough to come was Rotimi. He had stopped round the day before. The meeting had been quite weird.

He was having his morning coffee when he heard a slight knock on the door followed by Rotimi slipping into the room. Rotimi had a defiant expression and Adrian instinctively looked at his watch. It was not yet 7.

"Good morning, sir," he said, smiling lightly.

"Good morning, Rotimi. You are in pretty early this morning!"

"I knew I would find you alone this morning, sir. So I made an effort to come early."

"Okay," Adrian said, taking a sip from his coffee. "Do you want some coffee? Do help yourself."

"I'm okay, sir," Rotimi said. "How are you, sir?"

Adrian couldn't help but smile. It never ceased to amaze him how Rotimi could weave off statements like that. Steeped in an obvious respect and awe of Adrian, Rotimi was still familiar and casual in a way that often tickled Adrian. It must be his use of the term 'sir' that did it. No matter how many times Adrian had asked him to drop the pretentious title, he always continued.

"I'm very well, Rotimi," Adrian said. "So, how can I help you?"

Rotimi looked him bravely in the face and smiled nervously.

"I…I…want you to know, sir, that I will always be your

boy. You will always have my loyalty."

The statement had not only been unexpected to Adrian, he also did not know how to react to it. Talking of loyalty in this fashion made him uneasy. He wondered if there was not a plot against him, or a group of people working against his interest within the organization.

"Well, thank you, Rotimi. I don't know what to say."

"I don't care what anyone says about you, sir," Rotimi continued. "I don't even care if you are what they say you are… You are the best boss anyone could have."

Adrian realized that Rotimi had deliberately avoided using the term 'gay' or 'homosexual.' He was touched though by Rotimi's resilience and bravado in spite of all that was happening. Adrian had to blink back the tears threatening to cloud his eyes.

"Thank you, Rotimi. But you don't have to do this. I'm okay, and I don't want you to make unnecessary enemies here on my account."

"I wouldn't be here if it wasn't for you. You are my man."

That was the statement that most unnerved Adrian. It was its hidden implication. It was the tone in which it was said. Indeed it was simply everything about the statement itself. For the first time in years, Adrian felt a slight stirring in his loins. When Rotimi left his office, Adrian was afraid of himself. He spent the whole day playing back the incident in his head, trying to decipher its meaning and understand the emotion that had come over him.

Adrian was relieved when he hit the highway. There was little or no traffic. It was Saturday after all, so the roads were free but some Saturdays could be bad, depending on how many weddings or parties were taking place and where. Adrian was always infuriated when a road, major or not, was blocked off because some 'big man' was throwing a party, causing traffic to be diverted.

He stopped at a local car wash by Bar Beach to have his car cleaned. He was very conscious of appearance. He had to look good and organized in front of his family. There was no need to present himself as any less, or give the impression that he suffering since leaving home. He had to look strong and coordinated even though he knew inside he was a broken man, fighting with his inner demons.

While the half-naked youngster sponged his car into a lather, Adrian's eyes wandered off towards the debris-littered white sand of the beach. In the distance he could make out two horses being ridden by two individuals. One was a white man and the other black. The white man was kitted up in riding gear, complete with black leather boots and dark glasses to shield his eyes from the sun, while his companion was in tattered shorts and without shoes. He obviously was a stable help or something. It was the white man's gait that captured Adrian's interest. From a distance he looked like Antonio: tanned complexion, curly black hair that danced with the wind and covered his face occasionally. Antonio was the reason Adrian had promised himself to shut the door to his gay life. Antonio, the beautiful Spanish hunk to whom Adrian had once promised his heart; the one who had broken his heart. That was a long time ago. That was another life.

"Oga," the car wash man said, tapping Adrian's shoulder, "I don finish your car. I even shine am."

Adrian looked at the young man trying to make out what he had just said. It was obvious the lad was pleased with his work, judging by the wide grin on his face exposing a shocking set of pearly whites set against a dark sun-burned face.

"How much?" Adrian asked, putting his right hand in his trousers' pocket.

"Na two hundred, sir," the young man replied confidently.

Adrian paid him the money without arguing. He was happy with the wash and nodded his approval at the young man who smiled even wider and quickly ran off, flagging down a filthy-looking red Honda that was sure to be his next customer.

As Adrian drove off he found himself questioning his fascination with the man on the beach. Why was he thinking of things he had laid to rest for so long now? Why was he losing his focus? Today was going to be a good day. He was going to see his wife and daughter after a forced separation. He should be thinking of them.

But his heart was beating in panic now. He was experiencing anxiety and mixed feelings. There door was ajar in the closet he had sealed up in his mind years earlier, and all the memories in it were threatening to burst out, challenging him to confront his most private fears. Adrian was not ready to do so. He just wanted to see his family and try to work things out with his wife. A part of him was certain that he still wanted to remain married and accepted by society, but another part was fighting to be let loose and be confronted head on, demanding to be recognized.

As Adrian neared home, the confidence he felt earlier slowly faded away and left in its place doubts and uncertainty.

◉ ◉ ◉

WHEN ADA hung up the phone, she looked lovingly at her daughter and forced a smile. She had not anticipated Adrian demanding to come over and quite frankly did not know what to do when he got to the house. But Ego had cried for him all through the day before, and she had no choice but to call Adrian.

"Sweetheart," Ada said, "daddy is coming to see you today."

Ego squealed in delight and hugged her mother tightly. At the other corner of the room, Nkechi widened her eyes in surprise and her lips parted speechlessly.

"So run up to your room and get Isioma to dress you up, okay?"

"Yes, mummy." Ego rushed out of the living room.

As soon as she left the room, Nkechi walked over to Ada. She sat opposite her and held both her hands softly.

"Is it wise for you to let Adrian come here? I'm worried that you are not ready to face him."

"He wants to see his daughter. I can't deny him that and, moreover, Ego has been asking for him."

Ada understood Nkechi's concern. They had spent the whole morning discussing how they both had missed all the signs. Nkechi kept blaming herself for making the connection between Ada and Adrian. Ada tried to let her know that she was not a child and had pursued the relationship in her own right and made the decision to marry Adrian herself.

"I think you too should go up to your room and fix yourself up before Adrian gets here."

"Why?" Ada asked.

"Why!" Nkechi exclaimed. "You can't let him see you like this. You look sad and destroyed. What impression do you want him to have?"

Ada looked at herself. She was still in her rumpled nightdress and her hair was in a mess. She had in two days grown slightly leaner due to not eating and thinking too much, and she had bags under her eyes.

"The truth, Nkechi, is that I am sad and destroyed. Is it a crime to wear my pain on my face?"

"No sweetheart, it's not a crime. But you don't confront

him looking like you are defeated already. You have to do this for you and maybe some day you will thank me for this."

Ada knew she was right, but as hard as she tried, she could not see herself getting prepared, like Ego, to see Adrian. Just then she knew what she must do.

"I won't see him."

"What?" Nkechi said. "What do you mean, you won't see him?"

"I simply won't see him," Ada insisted. "He's coming here to see his daughter and not me."

"Okay," Nkechi shrugged in resignation, "don't see him if you don't want to, but go and take a bath and be presentable in case any other visitor shows up."

Ada did not argue with her. She made her way to her bedroom, disrobed and walked into the adjoining bathroom where she soaked her body in a warm foamy bath. The caressing of the water soothed, and she allowed her thoughts to wander off to that far-away place of almost forgotten yesterdays.

She didn't know when sleep took over until she heard the distant honking of a car's horn. She knew that particular sound. It was Adrian's Mercedes. Ada quickly jumped out of the bath and swung a lush robe on her wet, naked flesh. Shuffling fast, she entered the bedroom and made her way to the curtained window. She shifted the blinds lightly so she could steal a look at the gate down below. It was Adrian all right, and he was looking well and undisturbed. She even noticed his damned car was sparkling in the brilliance of the scorching sunlight.

Damn him! Ada cursed under her breath. She could not believe she was on the brink of an emotional breakdown, sick with worry while Adrian was looking so happy and healthy. She had hoped that he would be as broken as she was, haggard and weighed down with worry. That was the picture she had painted in her mind. She had hoped that she was not the only one suffering from all this.

As soon as she noticed his face lift up towards the bedroom window, Ada quickly dropped the blinds back in place and stepped away to avoid any possibility of being seen.

Nkechi had been right after all. She wasn't going to give him the benefit of seeing her in such a vulnerable state. She had to look equally undisturbed and strong. She had to let him know that she was capable of taking care of herself if it came down to that.

She moved over to her dresser and began applying make-up to hide the telltale signs of stress. The result was satisfying. She selected a form-fitting pair of light blue jeans and matched them with a flaming red, low-neckline blouse.

She listened carefully to the voices emanating from the direction of the living room. Moving closer to the bedroom door, she made out Adrian's sensual voice saying something, and Ego's accompanying squeak of delight. She shut her eyes tightly, fighting back the tears forming within her.

The door gently opened, narrowly missing Ada's head. She looked up to find Nkechi standing only inches away and staring at her.

"He's with Ego."

"I know. I can hear them."

"He asked for you. Maybe you should see him."

Maybe, Ada thought, but she could not trust herself with what she might say or do. She knew one thing though: she could not afford to cry in front of him or Ego for that matter. She turned away from her cousin and took successive deep breaths to calm her nerves.

"You look very beautiful, Ada," Nkechi said. "And I think you should face him and not hide like you are the guilty one."

Ada was not listening to her anymore. She moved back to her vantage point by the door to spy on Adrian and Ego. Adrian had her on his lap and was either telling her a story or promising some fantastic gift or journey. Ego loved travelling. They looked so happy that it hurt Ada to watch them together like that. Had she any right to put an end to that relationship? Worse still, did Ego feel that amount of love for her as well? She wanted to join them and be part of their love, but a much stronger instinct held her back. It was the part that kept telling her that this was not real, but make-believe.

There was a hiss from the far corner of the room. Ada turned to look at Nkechi who was now sitting on the bed with a bitter scowl on her face. Ada could only guess what she was thinking.

"Even if I were to confront him, what would I say? I can't say anything with Ego in there."

"At least show yourself. Sweetheart, you need to snap out of this self-pity and start thinking fast."

Ada was tired of thinking. She wanted all this to be a nightmare she was stuck in, from which she would soon awaken, her eyes bursting open like a flower pod kissed by the first dew of a new day. But she was still very angry, hurt and ashamed. It was this shame that troubled her. She was ashamed that she had made the wrong choice by marrying Adrian. She was ashamed that if this got out, everyone would sneer at her and wonder at her abject naïveté.

"I'm going out there and I'm taking Ego away with me to my house to play with her cousins," Nkechi announced, getting up from the bed. "You and Adrian will have to talk."

Ada watched her exit the room and she said nothing to stop her. Her body was not her own anymore. Her grief had taken over and left behind a shell. She didn't care if Adrian

wanted to see or speak with her. She only knew she would
let herself listen and then react accordingly. What would be
the proper way to react to such a situation anyway? She did
not know. She did not know any other woman who had
gone through a similar experience with whom to compare
notes. She probably was the only woman whom this had
happened to!

She peeked through the door again and witnessed
Nkechi's attempt to carry Ego in her arms and the brief
moment of argument that ensued between Nkechi and
Adrian who was obviously not happy with this development.
She noticed Ego start crying and reach out to her father,
but Nkechi whispered something fiercely to Adrian who
immediately fell quiet and did not further resist as Nkechi
walked out of the living room. After a minute or so, Ada
heard the soft noise of a car engine start and the grating
sound of moving tyres as a car pulled away. She was now
alone with Adrian.

In a moment of panic, she imagined Adrian forcing his
way into the bedroom and pleading with her to forgive and
love him and then before she knew it, they would be in bed
together making love and promising never to part again.
This picture did not appeal to Ada. She instinctively rushed
out of the bedroom, halting only momentarily by the foot
of the staircase to stare at Adrian who was by now on his feet
staring back. She wanted to speak, to say something to him,
but her tongue was tied up in twists making it impossible.

Her eyes were drawn to his bare hands on which
she could make out pulsing veins and curly black hairs;
those hands that had once caressed and held her. She
moved her eyes to his lips which were parted and lush in
their tenderness; those lips that had once kissed her and
whispered sweet nothings into her ears; those lips which
had lied to her and hid truths she dare not know or fathom.

Then their eyes met and she felt her throat constrict in a sudden panic.

"Ada," Adrian said, moving towards her, "how are you?"

Ada backed away from him and remained mute.

"Please talk to me," Adrian begged. "I know this has not been easy for you, but I'm also going through the same thing as well."

Ada sniffed and rolled her eyes.

Adrian understood her pain and reluctance to talk to him but wished she would just say anything at this point. The awkwardness of the situation made him uneasy being alone with her.

"I've come here today to explain to you about me, us and what happened," Adrian spoke slowly. "You must know that I never wanted to hurt you or anyone, but I did what I did because I saw no other way out."

"Why me?" Ada finally spoke. "Why did you make this happen to me... to us?"

These questions shocked Adrian and it showed.

"You make it sound like I planned all this. I had no choice, Ada."

"If you didn't plan this, then what do you call it? I don't care if you are gay, but you had no right to fool me and make me marry you."

"Excuse me." Adrian's voice rose in spite of his attempt to control his temper. "The truth is you did not have to marry me at all. You had a choice to walk away. I never expected you to have any interest in me but you did. I could not shake you off, even when I tried."

"So it's all my fault," Ada shot back. The sting of his last statement lingered. "You could have told me you preferred boys and I would have stopped calling you."

"I'm the same person, Ada. I wasn't seeing anyone when we got together."

"But you'd slept with men in the past," Ada responded.

"In the past!" Adrian stressed. "With you it was a new beginning. I was starting afresh and I never asked you questions about your past."

"I was a virgin, Adrian. I had no past to share with you and you put me at risk of HIV."

Adrian sighed. "Wake up, Ada. Straight people can contract HIV as well. What do you think, that it is exclusive to gay people? What would you have preferred, that I was a hopeless womanizer who had slept with hundreds of women?"

"I don't expect anything from you but honesty," Ada cried. "Would I have stuck around if I knew about you? The answer is I don't know. But it would have been my choice. Mine!"

The silence that ensued was pregnant with tension. Emotions were high and both of them knew they were on the brink of crossing that thin line between patching things up or destroying a family they had spent years building.

"I'm so sorry that I didn't tell you about me," Adrian said quietly and softly. "But that was a part of my life that I had shut the door to. I didn't want to revisit it."

"Why?" Ada asked. "Is it because you knew it was unnatural? A sin?"

"No. This is who I am. I had no choice in that aspect of my life. I'm not ashamed of it."

"Then why did you have to shut a door to who you are?"

"Because," Adrian whispered painfully, "I was hurt."

He turned away from her as soon as he uttered those words. He had been hurt, not unlike how she was hurt now, and he was acutely aware that he was responsible for her pain.

"You need to read your Bible, Adrian. Even God forbids

the act."

"Then let God be the one to judge me," he answered. "I was born this way. I wish you could only see that."

But she couldn't and feared she never would. Tears filled her eyes and at the same time a burning rage was rising within her. She wanted to scream, lash out at him, run away from him, all at the same time.

"Please go. I have nothing else to say to you."

"Ada, we have a family together," Adrian said. "We need to discuss what we intend to do now."

"I can't think right now," she cried. "Just go... go away and leave me alone."

Adrian didn't argue with her. He simply walked away. She watched him leave, his gait that of a defeated man. She felt no joy seeing him this way but she couldn't think of him even. All she could think about was herself.

◎ ◎ ◎

THE RUMOURS were rife at the reception party.

Iheoma had first got a whiff of the talk at the church ceremony. A cluster of four women dressed similarly in pink chiffon brocade and matching *gele* were discussing in an animated fashion. Iheoma recognized one of the women, Modupe Ajala-Osagie, the rich socialite wife of Chief Ibinabor Osagie, the oil magnate. Iheoma was not exactly a friend of Modupe's, but both women did their nails at the same beauty salon on the island and they normally exchanged nods and the occasional 'good day'. The other ladies in the group were not recognizable to Iheoma, but she guessed that they were either social climbers or minor society ladies hanging around Modupe.

Iheoma, not one to miss out on good gossip, made her way to the group of women with a warm smile on her face. Inside, she was cursing Ada for making her come to this wedding alone. She had been looking out for the other friends they had in common, but so far she had not been lucky enough to team up with anyone she was comfortable with. It didn't help that it was such a big wedding and it seemed like all the highly placed people in Lagos were there.

"Hello!" Iheoma smiled when she got to the ladies. "It's so nice to see you all here."

The ladies all smiled back at her, muttering hellos and other pleasantries. Iheoma was pleased that Modupe recognized her and even knew her name. It made sticking with the ladies a little more bearable. But after ten minutes, she got tired and bored. All she ended up gathering was that some poor woman's husband had been exposed as a cheat. Iheoma could not understand what was so fascinating about the story. This was Lagos after all; all the men here were cheats and the women were no better either. Many a society lady had been found in compromising situations with other married men. Of course news like that always made its way to the front cover of the various sleaze magazines, which were fully patronized by women like Modupe hoping they would be photographed in their latest attire and jewelry.

Iheoma was happy to excuse herself from the ladies. They didn't even share the name of the cheating husband or heartbroken wife with her. She didn't see any fun in the story if she could not identify its cast.

When she heard whispers of this story again at the reception party, Iheoma decided to take an active interest in it. She weaved her way into the midst of another group of ladies speaking in hushed tones.

"…the wife was supposed to be here today." One was saying.

"But are you sure he is?" another asked. "They looked like the perfect couple."

"My husband said it is true." Another whispered, "he works at DialPlus and they say one of those security men claimed he even made a pass at him."

"I think I heard of that one too," Iheoma chipped in with ease. "What is the man's name again?"

"The security man?" the wife of the DialPlus employee asked.

"No, the cheating husband," Iheoma said.

There was a hush as the ladies quickly looked around to make sure no one else was listening to them.

"Adrian Njoko!" one of the ladies whispered. "You know, that Ada's husband… She owns that very fashionable interior decor business. They did my kitchen for me last year. Can you imagine her husband is gay! Poor woman, do you know her?"

"Yes," Iheoma acknowledged, "I know her."

Iheoma stayed long enough to get the full details of the story and when none of the women was paying any more attention to her, she moved away.

There must be some truth to all this, she reasoned with herself. After all, there could be no smoke without fire and Ada had sounded worried the last time they had spoken and had pulled out from coming to the wedding. Her reason was family issues! This must be it! Iheoma said to herself. This was the reason Ada was asking her about being alone. Adrian was gay and Ada had found out.

Despite the noise from the party, Iheoma whipped out her cell phone from her purse and dialed Ada's number. The call wouldn't go through. She checked her phone screen and saw she had no signal at all. She cursed under her breath and found her way outside of the reception venue. The noise was less here, but still no signal. In frustration she began to run to the car park, hoisting her dress up so she would not trip and fall on her face. She was there in a minute and let out a cry of despair when she realized that her car was blocked off by other cars and she would not be able to drive out until the party was nearing its end.

She checked her phone again, and still no signal.

"Damn it!" she cursed. She had to get through to Ada somehow.

◉ ◉ ◉

THE NOISE of children playing in the backyard was beginning to get to Nkechi. They were singing, screaming and running round in endless circles without a care in the world. She remembered playing exactly like this as a child with her siblings. She remembered also when Ada used to come over for the holidays and join in their silly little games. Even then, she had so loved her cousin and always acted as her big sister. It had been so nice to be older than someone finally, and 'Little Miss Àthìngà', a name her older cousins and aunts had coined since Nkechi was so minuscule, helped fulfill Nkechi's sense of importance. But it had never bothered her really. Her parents had always made her feel like the most beautiful and wonderful child and she believed them. This was one of the reasons she had developed such a strong sense of self very early in her childhood.

Now, Nkechi inevitably felt like she had betrayed her cousin. She held herself responsible for Ada meeting Adrian and their marriage. She knew this line of thinking was to an extent unreasonable. After all, both Ada and Adrian were consenting adults and had made their own decisions.

She couldn't believe she had been so wrong about Adrian. He was a nice person. But he was gay! This was definitely not right. Being a strong Christian, she could not be tolerant of such behaviour. It went against all her morals and she could imagine what her pastor would say about people like Adrian.

Just then there was a loud scream and running feet. She looked up and saw Junior, her son, running past with a doll and, following him with tears in her eyes was Kamdi, his little sister. Ego was walking behind both with a confused look.

"What is it, Kamdi?" Nkechi asked.

"Junior took my doll again," she cried. "He's always playing with my dolls."

Something in Kamdi's comment triggered off an alarm in Nkechi's head. She had never taken much notice of it before, but it was now quite clear. Her son was always playing with his sister's dolls even though he had his own toys and football. He didn't have much interest in his toys and was usually too quiet and withdrawn. Was this how it all began? Was this how, if left unchecked, her son could become an Adrian?

Nkechi screamed at the top of her lungs. "Junior! Junior, will you come here right now!"

Her scream brought with it a chill. It immediately silenced the crying Kamdi and made Ego freeze where she was standing. When Junior slowly traced his steps back to the living room, he looked like he had shrunk into himself, cowering with the doll held out in his outstretched arms as if offering alms. Nkechi grabbed the doll from him and, without thinking, slapped him across the face with the back of her free hand.

"Boys don't play with dolls. Do you hear me?" She yelled harshly.

"Yes, mummy." Junior sniffled as tears rolled down his right cheek and he ran off to cry in his room.

"Here you go, darling," Nkechi said, offering the repossessed doll to Kamdi.

Kamdi did not move from the spot where she had been frozen when her mother hit Junior, neither did she reach out to take the doll. Her young mind could not understand the rage that had suddenly possessed her mother. Her mother had never hit any one of them in that fashion before.

"Kamdi, take your doll and go play with Ego."

"No." Kamdi shook her head and, as the tears formed in her eyes, she ran off in the same fashion and direction as Junior.

Nkechi was left standing with Ego by her side. Guilt washed over her as she noticed the terrified look in the child's eyes. She hadn't meant to snap at Junior like that or even hit him. She had acted out of fear. Now both her children were locked up in their room crying, and also in fear of her. She closed her eyes to fight back the tears building up and just then felt the doll being pulled out of her hand. Her eyes squinted open. Ego stood holding the doll close to her chest and rocking gently from side to side. Nkechi smiled at her and watched her walk away towards the children's room.

Later that night in bed with her husband, Obi, Nkechi could still not shake off the worry and anxiety plaguing her. If someone as normal-looking as Adrian was gay, then how many more men out there were living double lives as well? She had always thought gay men were effeminate and wanted to play girls. This was why she was worried about her son. He seemed too soft for a boy.

"What is the matter?"

"Nothing," she lied.

Obi pressed, "come on, tell me. Something is obviously worrying you. You've been tossing and turning all night."

"I hit Junior today," she blurted out.

"Why?"

"He was playing with Kamdi's dolls again." Nkechi

turned around so their eyes could meet.

"Again!" Obi said quizzically. "Nkechi, he is just a child. That's what they do – play."

"He is always playing with dolls," Nkechi stressed. "I never see him playing with the other boys outside. He has footballs and other toys but he prefers to play with Kamdi's doll."

"He will outgrow it, Nkechi. He's just a kid." Obi was trying to reassure her.

"He's eight years old. I'm afraid he is going to become like one of those sissies."

"What are you saying?" Obi whispered harshly.

"Have you ever wondered about how many homosexuals there are out there? If we as parents don't monitor our children and guide them in the right path, they could make the wrong choices later in life."

Obi sat up and, staring at Nkechi strangely.

"Are you saying our son is a homosexual?"

"I'm saying that our son is playing with dolls like a girl. And if we don't correct it now, he will carry on till he is in his teens and young adulthood, and one day he will be confused about his sexuality."

An uncomfortable and tense silence followed. Obi got out of bed and rested his head on the full-length mirror adjacent to the bed. He could not bear to look at his wife just that minute.

"*My son* is not a homosexual," he finally said between clenched teeth. "And don't you ever lift your hand to strike him again!"

Nkechi covered her face with her hands and began to cry. She wanted to tell him that she had every reason to be concerned. That she was responsible for her cousin being married to a homosexual. But she couldn't. She had promised Ada that she would tell no one, especially family members. How would he understand that their son was not acting the same as other boys of his age? She could not bear the thought of raising a boy who would turn out to not be a real man.

How could he possibly understand?

◎ ◎ ◎

AS SOON as she saw Iheoma coming out of her car, Ada knew she knew. There was a sense of urgency in the way she rushed towards Ada. There were so many questions in her eyes that even her professional make-up or glittering dress could not hide.

"How was the wedding?" Ada asked as they embraced.

"Sandra was so beautiful. She sends her love."

Ada led Iheoma into the living room and they both sat down together on the couch. She was acutely aware now that she would have to face the reality of this nightmare and either begin fending off questions or dealing with them one at a time. She would have to start now, as it was quite obvious that Iheoma had something to say.

"Ada, you should have told me."

Ada shrugged.

"What did you hear?"

"Is it true that Adrian is gay?"

"Was everyone talking about it already? God, how did they know?"

"Not everybody. Just a few women. You should know how news travels in this town. Is he in?"

"No." Ada fell back on the chair, sighing. "He moved out two days ago."

"Was he cheating on you?"

"No. It was just something from his past. But I don't know. Who can tell? He has lied to me from the very beginning so I can't tell what is true anymore."

Iheoma shifted uneasily on the couch. She took a deep breath and let it out in an audible sound. She knew what it was to feel betrayed. She had lived with it for most of her adult life and it had not been easy, especially with a child to take care of, but she had persevered and made her life a success story. If her life were to be rewritten, she would gladly skip the heartaches and betrayal all together. She would not want her friend to have to go through that awful journey.

"What does your heart tell you?"

"I don't understand."

"I mean do you have any reason to believe that Adrian cheated on you?"

"For eight years he has lied to me, Iheoma," Ada retorted.

"That doesn't answer my question."

"I don't know, Iheoma. I hope nobody asks me that question because I don't know the answer to that. I just can't be with Adrian right now."

Inside, Ada was burning with rage. After her meeting earlier with Adrian, she only wished that this ordeal would be over and she would wake up to a new perfect day. Now his sexuality was out in the open and she feared she might not be able to handle all that came with it. Would she still be able to hold her head up high and talk with confidence? Would she be as candid with other people as she had been with both Iheoma and Nkechi? Would people be able to notice her vulnerability?

Suddenly Iheoma was laughing loudly and uncontrollably, as if she were the keeper of a private joke. She was laughing so hard that tears flowed down her cheeks leaving a trail of black lines from her mascara.

"What is so funny?" Ada asked uncertainly.

"You are! The look on your face is unbelievable."

Ada groaned, not quite getting the punch line.

"It's not the end of the world, Ada. So your husband turns out to be a closet gay guy, so what?"

Ada did not find the idea the least bit amusing. She stared at Iheoma. She must be a little crazy.

"Ada, do you seriously believe that you are the only woman in Nigeria whose husband fancies other men?" Iheoma asked sardonically. "You have managed to build a strong home with a man who obviously loves you…I just find it ridiculous that you will throw it all away because of some silly indulgence of his in the past!"

"It is not an indulgence of his."

"Then what really terrifies you, Ada?" Iheoma asked. "Having a gay husband or dealing with what people are thinking and saying?"

This question embodied the true issues Ada had been battling with ever since she discovered that she was free of HIV. But it was also more complex. The issue of homosexuality was a topic never discussed in any civil setting she knew of, and was taboo where she came from. It was abnormal as far as Ada was concerned, and now her life was entangled with it against her wish. She feared becoming one of the 'new outcasts,' women rejected by society and scorned through no fault of theirs. And her daughter would have to also bear the stigma and the mocking of other children. These were the real issues Ada had to come to terms with.

She did not expect anyone, least of all Iheoma, to understand all this. She hardly understood it herself. It wasn't just a question of sacrificing a home or family, it ran deeper. There was the deception involved and the risk of Adrian going back to that lifestyle. There really was no answer to Iheoma's question, only a vague picture of what the future might be.

5

Night came swiftly, ushered in by a cool but forceful breeze which seemed to blow the daylight away and, in an urgent rush and with a loud whistle, brought dark grey clouds. In the far distance, dancing whirlwinds swiveled and gathered dust and debris in an ancient ritual that announced an impending downpour. There was a heavy feeling in the air, mirroring the pain and anguish in Adrian's heart.

Sitting in a far corner of a bar, shielded by opaque lighting and the haze of cigarette smoke from other patrons of the bar, Adrian sipped on a glass of soda, his eyes fixated on the wall. Scattered thoughts and images roamed in his head with no immediate meaning, but offering glimpses of a forgotten past that threatened to resurface and repossess him. He was fighting his internal demons in a battle. He did not know yet who the victor would be.

How did he get here? He did not know that either. He only remembered Ada rejecting him and asking him to leave. He had driven off, not thinking of where he was going or where to go, just driving and driving as far away from her as he could. She was hurt, he understood, but she was not ready to see any reason with him. They had taken vows to be faithful to each other and he had kept to his side. A huge sacrifice it was for him, but how could she understand that! One thing was clearer to him now after the intense soul-searching of the last couple of days: he was a 'gay' man. He had accepted to be judged by society and had been forced to hide the essence of who he was by getting married.

Why had he come here? Why to this very restaurant-bar? Champağne! This was quite a popular spot for the expatriate crowd and cognoscenti. It was also a discreet place where same-sex lovers met or connected. He had frequented this bar in the past, in his other life. It had been a ritual to come to Champağne every Friday night after work and on Saturday evenings as well, in the hope of finding that elusive love to last a lifetime.

Snapping out of his trance, Adrian looked around him for the first time that evening. Nothing had changed in Champağne. There was still a sprinkle of expatriate couples gathered in small groups enjoying the happy-hour. In other parts of the bar, couples were seated – black and white, black and black, the occasional Asian or Hispanic couples. In another corner, singles hung around, young social-climbing women executives and a larger number of very fashionable single men. It was within this select group that the gay men lingered, scouting the bar for a suitable lover for the night or for rich 'sugar-daddies' to take care of their needs. Yet still within this mix dwelt the 'pure souls'; the quintessential, closeted gay men who were in search of true love, not money, not a free ride, not a ticket to Europe or America. In this all-too-familiar setting, Adrian felt the gripping fingers of fear tug at him. Why had he come here?

At the far corner of the room, his eye caught with that of a dashing middle-aged man who seemed to be of northern descent. He was light-skinned. He looked regal in a grey jacquard kaftan. He smiled at Adrian and raised his glass up in acknowledgement. Adrian looked away quickly.

This was not right! He shouldn't be here. Something strong and magnetic had drawn him here despite his own wishes. The memories of the long-forgotten past filled his mind with such clarity. The men, the friends, the lies and the heartbreaks that he knew all too well.

"Good evening." A deep accented voice came from above Adrian. It was rich, with a hint of an expensive European education.

Adrian was forced to look up. He was immediately mesmerized by the same smiling face of the regal stranger. The man stood so close to him that Adrian could catch whiffs of his cologne.

"My name is Yahaya."

"Hello…," Adrian managed to reply.

"Nice place, isn't it? I've never seen you here before."

Adrian remained quiet. He knew this stranger was flirting with him and it bothered him to think he was so transparently gay.

"Is this your first time here?"

"In a long time, yes," Adrian smiled uneasily.

Yahaya returned the smile and took the seat beside Adrian. There was confidence and elegance in the way he carried himself. Adrian noticed this. All the while his conscience was screaming at him to get up and leave but he felt bound to his seat.

"What do you think of that crowd?" Yahaya pointed to the singles' crowd.

"The men or the women?"

There was a slight pause as Yahaya looked at him intensely as if contemplating the true meaning of his question. He smiled broadly and lit a cigarette, offering one to Adrian who promptly refused.

"Both. The women look desperate but the men are more desperate. They even spend more time putting themselves together than the women… Look at that one."

Adrian's eye followed the trail of Yahaya's long

manicured finger to a rather slim and tall man wearing very tight jeans and a form-fitting shirt. The man's hair was done up in cornrows and he wore lots of jewelry around his neck, wrists and fingers. The most outstanding aspect of his appearance was the way he walked. He practically sashayed round the room in a supermodel's strut, hips swaying. It was quite a sight. Adrian smiled in spite of himself.

"I see what you mean."

"I personally like my men subtle and polished," Yahaya said self assuredly. "Something like you."

The smile froze on Adrian's face. Yahaya's boldness was unexpected. He didn't believe he had been so far removed from the scene that now it was perfectly acceptable for men to be so open about their homosexuality. This was not the West! But then again, Yahaya looked like someone who had been exposed to western culture and was well adjusted to it.

"Do I shock you with my honesty?" Yahaya asked smiling widely.

"I'm a married man," Adrian asserted.

"So am I." Yahaya showed his wedding band to Adrian.

"But you just said you liked men."

"Yes. I like men and I'm married. It's just the way things are. What about you?"

This was too much for Adrian. He could not believe he was having such an intimate discussion with a total stranger. It was too ironic. Here he was battling with his homosexuality and seeking acceptance from those he loved the most while this stranger was totally comfortable proclaiming his sexuality and the fact that he was married as well. Two different worlds! How could this be? Where had he been while this sexual revolution was taking place?

He was violently jolted back to the present when he felt the stranger's warm hands drop on his, discreetly caressing his knuckles.

"I'm sorry," Adrian said as he pulled his hands away and stood up, "I have to go."

Yahaya in a flash withdrew his business card from his pocket and slid it across the table towards Adrian. Adrian picked it up politely and dashed out of the bar, his heart beating fiercely. He found his car, got in and sped off.

He was excited in a strange kind of way, but more confused than anything. This had not happened to him in a long time and he had almost forgotten the euphoria it brought. But it was also crazy, he reminded himself.

His hands were shaking as he drove and he was sweating profusely in spite of the air conditioning in the car. He had to stop. Adrian parked off a dirt road linking to a major street and got out. Not far off from where he stood was a little kiosk with a middle-aged man in it. Adrian felt a strong craving for nicotine; it must have been from inhaling so much smoke from the bar. He found himself moving towards the kiosk with a purpose. The man behind the counter hardly took any notice of him until he picked up a packet of cigarettes.

"Two-fifty," the man announced.

Adrian searched his pocket for money. He found a rough five hundred naira bill and gave it to the man. When he collected his change and put it back in his trousers' pocket, the outline of the business card handed to him at the bar grazed his fingers. Adrian withdrew his hand as if he had just received a jolt of electricity.

He tore open the packet of cigarettes and withdrew a fresh stick. Fingers shaking slightly, he put the stick between his lips, borrowed a lighter from the seller and lit the cigarette. As the smoke filled his lungs, Adrian felt a rush and release. At the same time he felt guilt and betrayal.

He dipped his hand into his pocket and withdrew the business card in his possession. He read the name on it and as he took the second drag from the cigarette, realized that he had not even given the stranger his name.

◙ ◙ ◙

CHIKA BATTLED with his inner demons, his guilt. It made him think deep and far into his past, looking for hidden clues in his childhood and long-forgotten issues of his adolescence. He dug deep into the recesses of his mind, trying hard to exonerate himself, grasping weakly at straws of reason or explanation but getting no answers.

He was locked up in his study and had left instructions not to be disturbed. He needed to do some serious soul-searching. And there was no selfish reason involved. The truth was he had not been too happy with the way Chiedu had reacted towards Ebele. He believed Chiedu should have been more sensitive. And there was also Ada's rage and disappointment. The way things were going he had no idea what was to become of Ebele's home and family.

His sense of guilt stemmed from the memories of their childhood. Ebele had always seemed to be the outcast. He was a lonely child and even at a young age, Chika had felt his loneliness and understood his pain. There were many times he could have spoken up for Ebele, but he hadn't. He had been afraid of being laughed at or, worse still, being treated the same way as his brother: ignored and forgotten.

As a child he had asked himself time after time why his elder brother was different. Why did he sneak off to their father's balcony every morning after their father had just taken a bath? Why was he so timid when asked a question? Why did he cry so easily? Chika had observed him on more than one occasion stealing away to cry. There was a whole mystery surrounding Ebele when they were children.

And then, there had been the nasty pranks they had

played on him, Chiedu and himself. One particular incident always stuck out in Chika's mind but he was sure Chiedu had by now forgotten all about it. This was the night they had pushed Ebele down the cellar, enclosed in that worn-out carton.

Chika remembered the bone-crushing noise that lasted the entire period Ebele tumbled down the hard concrete stairs. He remembered vividly Ebele's muffled cry of pain and his anguish and fear as he watched helplessly. He had wanted to stop Chiedu from proceeding with the devious prank but he had kept quiet. He had said nothing.

Another episode of their childhood haunted Chika now even more than ever. He remembered so well that hot day. He had just returned home after a fun-filled afternoon of bike riding with his friends. He had been very angry and even spending hours with his friends had not helped quench the fire burning within. His anger was directed at his father. He had been promised a new bicycle the last time he was home from boarding school, and when he reminded his father that morning about the promise, he had been shouted at and told to manage what he had. How could he manage his outdated contraption of a bike? All his friends were riding new Raleigh bicycles while he had to bear the indignity of his cranky chopper. It was unacceptable and he felt like getting back at his father for this.

It was then a thought occurred to him. Both parents were out but their room was open. They never locked their room when they were out. After putting away his bike in the storeroom, Chika snuck into his parents' room. He closed the door behind him and quickly made his way to the closet. He knew where to look. In the third drawer by the right hand side was a wooden case where his father kept money. He found the box easily and, opening it, revealed a stack of neat naira notes and some foreign bills as well.

Chika's heart was beating fiercely now. He had never before in his life done anything like this, and yet he had no idea of what he was doing or intending. A strange had possessed him and it was as if he was no longer in control of his body or actions. He grabbed a handful of bills, stashed it hurriedly inside his pocket, replaced the box carefully and fled the room. No one had seen him. Later when he was alone in his room and felt bold enough, he brought out the money to count exactly how much he had taken. He was astonished at the amount: fifty naira! In 1982 that was very big money. Another fifty, and he would be able to get himself a new bicycle.

What was he going to do with all the money? He had to tell someone, but not Chiedu. He wouldn't want to lose any respect Chiedu had for him and of course he could certainly not report himself to their parents. He decided to tell Ebele.

"Give me the money so I can return it," Ebele cautioned. "There will be trouble if dad finds out."

"I'm not returning it," Chika said defiantly. "And you can't tell anyone about this."

"What will you do with the money then?"

Chika shrugged. He still had a scowl on his face.

"I can give you some."

"No thank you. I don't want any of it."

As predicted by Ebele, there was indeed trouble when their father found out about the missing money. It was two nights after the money was taken and Chika remembered that there had been no electricity so it was a very hot and dark night. After dinner, their father gathered all three boys in the living room with his animal-hide whip and a very angry look in his face. Their mother stood by the doorway, hands crossed and watching. One could cut the tension in the darkened room with a knife.

For some reason their father was staring solely at Ebele even when he addressed them all, demanding that the thief own up. Looking round quickly, Chika realized that their mother was also staring at Ebele. In a panic he knew he was doomed, he knew Ebele would reveal the real thief to them all and thus for a day secure the title of the most beloved. He cursed himself silently for disclosing his deed to him.

"I am not raising criminals in my home," their father said, "and I have never in my life stolen anything either. I want the three of you to tell me who took money from my room."

The brothers all stared at one another accusingly; only Chika knew that the look Ebele shot him was one of silent pleading. His eyes begged Chika to confess and save them all from the agony of this inquisition. Chika looked away and focused his eyes on his fingernails.

"Chiedu," their father called out, "did you take money from my room?"

"No," Chiedu answered with a touch of disgust in his voice.

Their father eyed him with some restraint.

"Ebele," he continued harshly, "was it you?"

Ebele said nothing.

"Ebele!" their father threatened.

"Yes, daddy," Ebele said in a small voice. "Chika... I told Chika I would return it."

That was a day Chika would never forget. After he and Chiedu had been dismissed, they could not shut their ears to the screams emanating from their father's bedroom while Ebele was whipped and punished, nor could they ignore his plea for forgiveness. Every stroke they heard left an unforgettable imprint on Chika's conscience. Every scream echoed in his head for many nights afterwards. And later that night when Ebele lay covered and shivering on his bed, Chika had gone to console him.

"I'm sorry. Why did you do it?"

He felt Ebele shivering underneath the cover and whimpering. He lifted the cover gently and was shocked at the sight of thick welts on his body, some weeping and oozing blood.

"We have to return the money," Ebele cried. "Do you still have the money?"

"Yes," Chika answered and strings of tears ran down his left cheek. "I still have the money."

"I have to return it to dad," Ebele said. "Give me the money."

Chika ran to his side of the room and retrieved the money he had taken from where he had hidden it, under his mattress. He rushed back to Ebele's side and squeezed the money into his palm.

"Thank you," he whispered into his ears.

The very next day while he was accompanying their mother to the market she remarked unexpectedly in the taxi, "Ppease, make sure you don't follow in the footsteps of your brother, Ebele."

Guilt squeezed the lifeblood in his heart.

"Can you hear me, Chika?" she pressed. "Make sure you never steal anything, okay?"

"Yes, mummy."

He got his bicycle on that trip and for the rest of the holiday Ebele was grounded. He never understood why Ebele had allowed himself to take the blame for the missing money. They never discussed it again and Chika never told a soul the truth.

He had to live with the guilt of knowing Ebele had not deserved the beating he got that day. It seemed, after that day, that Ebele became more of a recluse. He had always been different and Chika knew this. But you don't hate people because of they are different, do you? Chika asked himself. He realized that Ebele's oddness as a child had been a source of concern and fear for their family. Why else would their parents have pointedly ignored him? And his brothers too. They had made him invisible and he had become so. He was a sissy! And everyone hated a sissy. He cried easily, he was too frail and he wasn't just like either of his brothers. All this did not make him gay, but Chika had somehow known. There was always the suspicion.

Chika had always been closer to Chiedu and with time they both had drifted apart from Ebele. They had their lives to live, and Ebele did not fit into the picture. It didn't help that Chika had never felt comfortable around his wife, Ada.

All that didn't matter now. Chika was bent on supporting Ebele no matter what path he chose to walk. But he prayed silently that his choice would include his wife and lovely daughter, Ego.

Chika picked up his phone and dialled Chiedu's number.

"Hello, Chiedu," Chika said as soon as Chiedu answered his phone. "We have to talk about Ebele."

"I know," Chiedu said from the other end. "I've been thinking a lot since the last time we met."

"So have I."

There was a pause on both sides. Chika could hear Chiedu's breathing.

"I think we have been too hard on him."

"Why do you say that?"

"He has never really been a part of us," Chika answered. "He has always been different. Quiet and reserved when we were little. We never tried to really know him."

"That's not true," Chiedu defended. "That has nothing to do with his claiming to be gay."

"Chiedu, Ebele isn't claiming to be gay, he is gay. And if

you are really true to yourself, you will admit that you have always suspected."

Chiedu sighed.

"What can we do to support him?"

"We have to pray for him," Chiedu answered. "I will give him a call and invite him over. I'm expecting a visit from Pastor Matthew and some of the church brothers."

"I don't know about that. I don't believe Ebele would want anyone other than the family discussing this issue," Chika said uneasily.

"That's rubbish. I have already informed Pastor Matthew about this and he promised to come speak to Ebele. He told me he had had some success with issues like this. Apparently our brother is not the only man who has been sexually confused."

"I'm not really sure about this, Chiedu."

"Don't worry, everything will be all right."

Chika worried nonetheless. There was something not quite right with the whole arrangement. He believed Chiedu had been holding back something important as well. He had heard Pastor Matthew had a hard-line approach that the church found unorthodox.

After Chika hung up, he wondered what kind of success Pastor Matthew alluded to and what methods he employed to help the so-called sexually confused men.

◉ ◉ ◉

ADRIAN WAS fast asleep in the guest bedroom. Abdul had just poked his head through the door to make sure he was comfortable. He breathed a sigh of relief to see him all snuggled up underneath the comforter. He shut the door carefully behind himself and gently tiptoed away till he got to the living room where Femi sat watching television, his hands wrapped round a warm mug of cocoa. He shot Abdul an enquiring stare.

"How is he? Asleep?"

"Finally!" Abdul exclaimed.

Abdul dropped on the sofa and made to grab Femi's mug. Femi moved his hands away playfully and smiled.

"I made a cup for you too." He montioned to the big black mug on the coffee table.

"Thanks, honey. This is good," Abdul announced, after taking a sip.

He was exhausted himself and needed sleep, too. When Adrian had turned up hours earlier with his luggage and a lifetime worth of worries and guilt, he had no choice but to let him in with a promise that he could stay for as long as he cared, and that he would have an unfailing ear to hear all his woes. Adrian was in bad shape and what was more significant to Abdul was that he was smoking again. That was not a good sign.

He had always admired Adrian's strong will. From the minute he had made up his mind to stop smoking, Adrian had stuck to it. Something stronger than his will had broken his friend's resolve. When Adrian closed the door to his homosexuality all those years before, Abdul totally believed he had thrown the key away, never to revisit that part of his life again. But that evening, Abdul was no longer sure if Adrian hadn't found that old key or a spare, and was debating whether or not to let loose the part of himself he had denied for so long.

It was painful to see his friend in such a state. When Adrian rang his bell that evening and Femi answered the door, what stood in front of them was a shadow of the person they knew as Adrian. He stood there with his bags, soaking wet from the rain, his eyes wild like a beast. There was a lost look in his eyes, a pained look filled with desperation.

"Hey!" Abdul said. "It's okay, you hear?" You can stay here."

"I am so confused," Adrian cried, his body rocking with the force of his tears. "What have I done?"

Abdul pulled him in and signalled to Femi to lock the door behind them. As soon as Adrian was seated, his eyes zeroed in on the packet of cigarettes on the table and he grabbed it. Abdul was shocked but refrained from saying anything; instead, he helped Adrian with a lighter as soon as he had a stick in his mouth.

"Thank you," Adrian said puffing on the stick, "you are a good friend."

Abdul took a stick and joined him.

"I went to see Ada today. She called and said Ego wanted to see me. I thought we could work things out but she was so cold. My God, if you could only see the hate in her eyes!"

"She is hurt. She will heal with time."

"It was more than that," Adrian argued. "She thinks I've ruined her life. How could I have when I haven't been with anyone else but her?"

There was a pause right then and Femi joined them in the living room. Abdul had told him about Adrian's last visit, so he knew the dilemma their friend was in.

"I can't lose my family. I've worked so hard to have what I have today. I've had to make so many sacrifices. I had finally found some acceptance in my sad life and now this!"

"Your life is not sad. And it's not the end of the world."

"Yes it is," Adrian spat back.

"Why is this so important to you?" Femi asked.

Adrian took a long drag from his cigarette while he pondered that question.

"Because," he said finally, "for once in my life I was no longer Ebele, the scared little boy who was seeking acceptance and wanting to be noticed. I had my own family who adored me."

"But," Femi added in a low tone, "they didn't know the real you. They only knew the part you wanted them to know. Now they know you and will have to make a choice."

Abdul shot Femi a cautionary stare that warned him not to further aggravate the situation. They allowed Adrian to moan about how life had been so unfair to him. He vented his anger on society, his family, his wife and finally himself.

Abdul had never seen Adrian like that before. He was afraid that he was on his way to an emotional breakdown. The last time he had seen Adrian close to such a state was when he broke up with Antonio. Adrian had discovered that Antonio had been sleeping with one of his closest friends, a friend Adrian had actually introduced to Antonio. The rejection was too much for Adrian to bear at the time and had led him to reject men and instead pursue a heterosexual relationship.

"You won't believe where I was tonight," Adrian said after a while.

"Where?"

"Champagne."

Both Abdul and Femi gasped audibly which made Adrian smile.

"Oh Adrian, please don't tell me…"

"Don't worry," Adrian said, cutting Femi off, "I didn't do anything. I just found myself there after I left Ada. I don't know what made me go there. It hasn't changed much."

"Except the gay scene isn't what it used to be years ago," Abdul added. "The men are now bolder."

"I know what you mean. I got hit on tonight. As shocked as I am, when I look back at it I'm sort of glad that gay men are finally coming out of hiding. I'm not talking about the divas who are so loud and so effeminate, but the good-looking professional-types."

Recalling the conversation, Abdul was more convinced about what he perceived to be happening. Adrian was thinking of coming out again. Abdul had seen this so many times over the years. He had attended ex-lovers' and many other gay friends' weddings and he had listened to all of them condemn their past relationships with other men and even preach the gospel of heterosexual love; but months into their married life, they would sneak off to the usual joints by the beach or other discreet night spots to pick up men. After a year or two of marriage they all came clean to their gay friends, praising the 'new emerging breed of gay men' as the reason for their rebirth. It was different with Adrian, Abdul knew. Adrian was simply reacting to rejection once again but it had the same result.

It was such a relief that Adrian was now asleep. He had seemed determined to keep talking as if to purge his soul of all the guilt that had built up within him for the previous six years of his life. He lamented his love for his wife, his child and the perfect life he believed he had. He worried about his renewed craving for men. He cursed his abject weakness in the face of rejection.

After an hour of ranting with no end in sight, Adrian finally started showing signs of sleep. He was led to the guest bedroom. He had talked a bit more after that, but finally drifted off to sleep to Abdul's relief.

"What do you think?" Femi asked, as he and Abdul got ready to retreat to their bedroom.

"That is one troubled man. If only he could embrace his sexuality, he would be better."

"I think he's on his way there."

He may well be, Abdul pondered silently, as he shut the door to their bedroom.

◉ ◉ ◉

HE WAS in his old bedroom. The one he had lived in for the most part of his childhood and youth. It was a small room with a small bed, a wooden cupboard and a study table and chair. The ceiling fan still made that squeaky sound when it was on and the mosquito netting on the window by the top of the bed prevented him from sticking his head out to watch as life happened.

The door slowly blew open and he caught the familiar filter of voices coming from the living room below. He knew those voices. He knew there were four people in the living room. His father, mother and another couple. He knew that the couple had an uncanny resemblance to his parents. He also knew that they were not related. He knew that in the next few minutes his mother was going to come fetch him and ask him to join them in the living room. He knew this because he had been here before, at this very time, this very moment.

He spent the next couple of minutes soaking up the familiar smell from his old room; feeling the texture of his old blanket and smooth polished surface of his reading table. There was a strong senseof nostalgia that brought with it painful memories.

Like clockwork, his mother was tapping on his door. She wasn't smiling. Her eyes concealed guilt and regret.

"Ebele," she said, "I want you to come meet some people in the sitting room."

"Yes mummy."

She entered his room and scrutinized him with a critical eye, watching out for flaws.

"Tuck in your shirt," she ordered, "and make sure you comb your hair."

"Yes mummy."

He tucked in quickly and picked up the comb that lay strategically on his reading table, as if it anticipated this very moment. He dragged the comb through his coarse pepper-seed curls, wincing at the pain as it pinched and pulled at his scalp. When his mother was satisfied with his appearance, he stopped combing and followed her out of the room room.

"Walk straight," she commanded without even looking back, "don't slouch."

"Yes mummy."

When they got to the living room they were there just as he expected; the couple that bore a vague resemblance to his parents. They were smiling at him and had that proud expectant look in their eyes. He greeted them as was expected of him.

"Ebele," his father said, "sit down."

He obeyed. He knew what was coming next. He had been there before.

"Ebele," his father continued, "I want you to meet your real parents."

These were the very same words he had heard countless times. He never got beyond that point before the room began spinning out of control and he woke up drenched in sweat. It was the very same dream he had been having ever since he was a child. He couldn't remember now when exactly the dreams started but they had stopped many years before. Tonight, the dream had returned unchanged.

Adrian checked his wristwatch for the time and was amazed to learn it was almost noon. He stumbled out of the room and was greeted by the smell of freshly brewed coffee. He found Abdul and Femi in the small dining area, seated by a tall oval glass table with three high stools suitable for a company of three only.

"Good morning," Adrian said as he joined them.

"How do you feel today?" Abdul asked, pouring him a cup.

"Fine," Adrian took a sip from the mug handed over to him. "I had a horrible dream last night."

"The one where your parents introduced you to your real parents?" Abdul asked.

"Yes," Adrian paused before realizing he had told Abdul this dream in the past.

"Have you made up your mind what you will do next?" Femi asked.

"I really don't know."

"What about all the stuff you said last night?"

Adrian shrugged.

"I can't remember anything I said last night."

"Adrian, you have to come to terms with the fact that your wife may not want you back. You can't continue to be in denial. You have to learn to love yourself and embrace who you are."

"I love myself," Adrian said defiantly.

"Why do you think you had that dream last night?" Abdul asked, changing the subject.

"I don't know. That dream always freaks me out. When I was little, I often wondered what life would have been like if I was indeed introduced to another set of parents who would love me."

"Do you know what I think?" Abdul said.

"What?"

"You are still scared of your parents and desperately want their approval. Theirs is the one love you can't do without."

Adrian opened his mouth to respond but no words came out. He slowly closed it and looked away. There was a truth to Abdul's deduction that sent a chill down his spine. His parent's love and approval were two things he had secretly coveted all his life. He had wanted to be the son that they could be proud of and show off to their friends.

This had been so important to him while growing up. He had not been the brightest child in school and every prize-giving day, he looked with longing as either or both of his brothers were called up to receive prizes for sports or academics. He eventually won a prize in his fifth year of primary education for being the smartest pupil, and it was so big a surprise to him that he thought it was a mistake. So surprising was his win that even his parents did not know how to react. Ironically that year neither of his brothers won a prize. But in spite of this, his success was not celebrated, not in the way his brothers' had been. There was no lifting up in the air, no promise of new toys, no special dinner planned with his favourite dish and soft drinks. Nothing! That hurt him so badly. All he got was a handshake from his father and an uncomfortable comparison.

"Next time, try to aspire to be the most intelligent pupil in your set, just like Chika was." And so year after year, he had tried to be the best at something academic, but hard as he tried, he could never be the perfect son.

"Adrian," Abdul said pulling him out of his journey into the past, "are you okay? You've been staring straight for over five minutes now."

"I was just thinking about what you said. And I have to admit, I've spent my entire life waiting for my parents' approval."

Femi laughed. "We all look for approval from someone, whether they are our parents, employers, colleagues or whatever. It's nothing to be embarrassed about."

"I'm not embarrassed. I'm only amazed at how much of my life I have wasted waiting…"

And that was so true. He knew he had spent so much of what he called life waiting for a nod that may never come. He hadn't even thought about what the rest part of his life would be like if he never got their approval. Life would go on and he would heal. As much as he wanted to believe this mantra, he knew that he wanted to be whole. And being whole meant being accepted by his parents with open hands.

6

That morning started with a promise; a promise of cool breeze to make light the harsh rays of the sun that had scorched the flesh for days now. It was certainly a promise of better things to come. This sudden change could only be attributed to the rain of the night before. For those who were not caught up in the downpour, it had offered blissful intermission from the uncomfortable heat.

Waking up, Ada felt very refreshed. It was like she had no worries in the world as she stretched and yawned. It felt like old times; waking up with Adrian beside her, he would be reading a copy of the dailies and would urge her to go get the household ready for church. She had always loved this Sunday morning ritual. Adrian was not by her side this morning, but she had not felt that pinch of regret which seemed to mark her every waking hour for the last couple of days. There was a change in the air. Yes! Certainly a change and she was not going to fight it. She was simply going to go with the flow and enjoy the mystery of the unexpected.

As she got up and began straightening her bed-cover, she wondered if her sudden perkiness owed itself to the fact that Iheoma had persuaded her to follow her to an all-girls get-together. She surprised herself when she easily acquiesced to Iheoma's request, but was secretly pleased that she did. Iheoma was a load of fun and outings with her always ended up being hilarious. And she needed something to lift her spirits. She wanted to laugh again. She wanted to be alive again. She was glad that Nkechi had decided to have Ego spend the previous night with her.

In the bathroom, Ada decided against having a bath and settled for a long shower instead. As the warm water beat down on her, she grabbed a bar of soap and worked it on her body till she was covered in soapsuds. When she touched the outline of her breasts, she felt a tingle, a longing. She closed her eyes and, throwing out all the doctrines from her strict Christian upbringing, slowly but tenderly caressed herself, following the trail of the warm water until she was cradling the essence of her womanhood. Touching, feeling, probing until a quiet sigh escaped her hungering lips. She had never felt such intense release before and she was overcome by shame. She rushed through the rest of the shower.

However, determined to have a good time that day, Ada resolved to block out her shame from the shower. Today was not a day to feel any part of guilt. She wasn't going to let anything spoil the frame of mind she had woken up with.

"You look wonderful, Ada!" Iheoma screamed when she saw Ada later that morning. "My God! You can still pull some twenty-something boys who don't know you are a mother of a big girl. Na wa for you o!"

"Stop teasing me. You haven't told me where you are taking me to and who would be there."

Iheoma laughed. "Ada, you worry too much. We are going to Carol Obosi's house. You know Carol, don't you? She's playing host to us for lunch with two other ladies, Hajiya and Temi."

"Yes, I know Carol," Ada said rolling her eyes.

"Why the face?" Iheoma asked.

"It's nothing," Ada answered. "You know how I feel about Carol."

"Yes I do and you know what I feel about that," Iheoma admonished. "You are just being a snob."

"No I'm not!"

When they got to the grand architectural edifice on Queens Drive, Ikoyi, a structure that overlooked the ocean and was barred off by an equally imposing fence and guarded by two armed military men, Ada sighed at what she had always considered opulent waste. The armed guards recognized Iheoma and let them drive in.

In the foyer, a stale scent of cigarette smoke lingered potently in the air. When the very flamboyant Carol made an appearance, it seemed she floated in, in a cloud of cigarette smoke, wearing a peach-colored boubou that did make her look like an eternal butterfly. She was of course smoking, a habit Ada personally abhorred. Ada was from the old school that did not believe it was responsible for women to smoke.

Carol was the-ever gracious host. She hugged both women and led them to one of the three grand living rooms. There, they joined the other ladies who had arrived earlier. It was quite a high profile mix of women Ada had come to discover. Carol was married to Major Obosi who had been a minister during the military era and still remained one of the wealthiest, controversial figures now. Hajiya's husband was in the current government as a special adviser to the minister of petroleum, and Temi's husband, Adebayo George, was a high-ranking judge in the Supreme Court.

Ada was not easily intimidated by other women but had to wonder why Iheoma had chosen this set to spend her Sunday with. As far as Ada was concerned, she had nothing in common with any of them. Their substance was solely attributed to their husbands' wealth, which was questionably obtained, and none worked for a living. In spite of her reservations, Ada made a wonderful effort to be attentive to all that was said, laughed at all jokes and even contributed to the conversation by sharing funny anecdotes with the women, while discreetly giving Iheoma an exasperated look. Iheoma returned her look with one of her own that simply said, "Behave!"

"So Ada," Carol said in the middle of lunch as she faced her squarely, "I've heard the rumour about your husband."

Ada's eyes widened in shock.

"Come now, my dear, you don't have to look so shocked," Carol added. "This is a gathering of friends and we can be open with each other."

Ada looked desperately from Iheoma to Carol. She was still speechless. She definitely was not ready for this. She wanted the ground to open up and swallow her, so no one could see her shame. Her heartbeat increased and there was a loud thundering noise in her ears as a feeling of isolation engulfed her. For a moment it seemed the scene had dissolved around her, leaving only an enormous void, with her on display and the other women sitting far off as judge and jury.

"Ada, please do not be alarmed," Carol said. "We are all here because we have a common issue. With the exception of Iheoma, we are all married to gay men."

Temi said smiling knowingly. "That's true. Bayo is gay."

"So is my Awwal," Hajiya chipped in quietly.

This revelation had the adverse effect of making Ada all the more nervous. Was she about to be initiated into a secret society of women with gay husbands? This was certainly how it felt and at that moment she could not decide whom she hated more: herself for agreeing blindly to follow Iheoma here or Iheoma for putting her in this position.

"Are you okay?" Carol asked.

"Yes I am," Ada replied. "It is all a shock to me right now."

"It always is my dear. You can imagine how I felt when

I first found out about my husband."

Ada asked in spite of her shock. "How did you find out?"

"I wasn't spared anything," Carol laughed as she lit a cigarette. "I came home early one day and there he was on the couch with a young man. I should have suspected something was wrong when his bodyguard almost stopped me from entering the compound. I threatened to have him fired before I was allowed to enter my own house."

"Were they…" Ada was horrified at the mental picture she had conjured.

"Yes they were, my dear," Carol laughed infectiously. "I was so shocked that I just stood there watching the whole act. When he finally noticed me, he made no apologies. The young man looked frightened. It is so funny thinking about it now."

Ada was clearly confused about Carol's general reaction. Why was she laughing? Why was the whole episode comical to her? Ada would have expected to see signs of grief, regret and anger, like she was feeling, but this woman seemed to be in a different world altogether. Was this what they called denial or was it just an acceptance of circumstances? Whatever it was, Ada could not comprehend the woman's ease and candour.

"I knew before I married my husband," Hajiya stated matter-of-factly.

"You did?" Ada turned to face her. "How come?"

"I was betrothed to Awwal when I was quite young," Hajiya said. "Even before I moved to his house as a wife I had heard about him and the boys. My first night with him, he invited one of his boys to our bed and he promptly told me what he liked. He was much older than I was so I could not argue or complain."

"I also knew about Bayo before I married him," Temi

said confidently. "In fact, that was the only reason I married him."

"I don't understand. Why?"

"Well," Temi said shyly, "the truth is, I'm not into men at all. I like women myself and by marrying Bayo, who knows of my preference, I am free to have my lovers while he has his. I don't care much for children."

Ada sat frozen on her seat. She could not believe all she had just heard. These three beautiful, educated women were comfortable being married to gay men! One of them was even admitting to being a lesbian herself. This was really too much for Ada to take in. What had happened to the old values they were all brought up with? A man and woman made up a family and then produced children, not a man and man or woman and woman. When had this foreign mentality creeped into Nigerian society?

"How have you managed to remain married to these men?"

"Simple!" Carol said. "As long as my husband provides me with all the comfort I deserve without complaint or compromise, then he can do whatever. I have a very influential husband who cares about his public image as much as I care about my luxuries. So my remaining married to him satisfies a social and political need."

Hajiya confirmed. "It's almost the same for me. I'm not the only wife, but all my needs are well taken care of. I travel a lot and have a separate account."

"I have my own money," Temi said. "I don't need Bayo for material wealth, my family is rich. For me what I enjoy is keeping my lover while he has his. To the world, we are the perfect couple and it serves its purpose politically as well, since he is a senior advocate."

"And you all sleep with your husbands?"

"I'm still his wife," Carol said.

"When he wants me," Hajiya said.

Temi simply shrugged.

Ada shut her eyes as she tried to absorb it all. Her temple was throbbing and she felt the world was coming to an end. These women were unbelievable. She wasn't a thing like any of them.

"Ada," Iheoma's voice broke into her thoughts, "you see, you are not alone in this."

Ada excused herself just then without replying Iheoma and fled to the nearest restroom. She shut herself in one of the stalls and sat on the toilet seat, resting her elbows on her knees so she could support her face in her hands. She was afraid to think. What was the world coming to if women could admit their lesbianism and marry bisexual men who still slept with them? And what was their lame reason for this madness? Comfort! Money!

There was a knock on the door before Iheoma opened the door and entered the room. It was a big room with two separate toilet stalls, like the ones seen in classy hotels. Ada was locked within one of the stalls.

"Ada! Are you all right?"

"Why did you bring me here?"

"I thought you would feel better knowing that you are not the only person with this peculiar problem. There are thousands of women like you scattered round the country."

Ada came out of the compartment she had been hiding in. Her eyes were red with anger and embarrassment.

"Those women are nothing like me. How could you even think that?"

Iheoma retorted; "Oh, Ada! Get off your high horse and realize that you are no better than these women. They've all had to deal with the same issue you are faced with and whatever way they choose to manage the situation is up to them. What you should learn from them is not to play victim. You have to pick up from where you are and continue."

"My God," Ada cried in a whisper, "these women are focused on status and money. I'm nothing like that. Temi is a lesbian, Iheoma! I'd never been so shocked in my life."

"Forget Temi," Iheoma said. "I only wanted you to meet her so you know women too could be gay."

"I know that, Iheoma. I went to an all-girls boarding school and know what some of the girls were up to but that was simply because there were no men around, and they all went back on holidays to meet their boyfriends."

"Oh I see," Iheoma said. "It's okay for women to be lesbian so far they are isolated with no male interference."

"I didn't say that."

"But you implied it. So long as those girls went back to their boyfriends you don't seem to be put off by the idea."

"I didn't say that," Ada repeated.

"And what about Carol and Hajiya? They found out the hard way but they are still living their lives."

"What kind of life is that?"

"They are living," Iheoma stressed. "They refuse to be victims. You have a daughter to think about as well; it's not all about you."

"So this is why you brought me here?"

"Ada, I brought you here for you to know there are countless other women out there dealing with this issue. Some choose to stay with the men, others choose to walk away and make new lives for themselves. Don't let this destroy you. Choose to be happy and live."

The room fell silent. Only their breathing could be heard.

"Let's go back and join the ladies so they don't take us for rude," Iheoma finally said.

Ada reluctantly followed Iheoma back to join the

women but it was hard to remain calm and objective after all she had heard. The rest of the afternoon was filled with more revelations for Ada. A whole new world was exposed. She learned of famous politicians, top government executives and other successful businessmen who were gay and married. She learned of their wives, those who were aware and those who weren't. She also learned of some of the lesbian women who were influential in society. It was all so shocking. The world had indeed evolved around her and she had missed it all.

By the time Ada left that evening, it seemed scales had been scraped from her eyes. It was like she began to see things in their true, stark colours: not simply black or white, but all the grey as well. As they drove past the waterfront, she took notice of the little things she normally took for granted; the way people dressed, spoke and carried themselves suddenly seemed so western and sexualized.

Ada was not sure if she welcomed such developments. The women she had just met also symbolized this evolution and they embraced it wholeheartedly. Could she be as open-minded as they were? She doubted it. But as Iheoma had pointed out, she also had her daughter to think about, and growing up with both parents was very important to a child.

Ada refused to think that night as she lay down to sleep. As her eyes finally succumbed to sleep, she willed herself not to dream…

◎ ◎ ◎

SHE DID not dream.

It was a relief to Ada when she woke up the next morning and realized that she had fallen into a deep slumber that was as clear as a plain sheet of drawing paper. She hoped faintly that when she woke up, she would discover that her meeting with the women of the day before had never happened. She would wake up and find out that it was Sunday all over again and she could have an alternate day ahead of her. But it was Monday. It felt like a Monday. The need to get up and prepare for work tugged at her. The silent hope that she could get one more hour of sleep, just one more hour, tempted her to return to bed. But there was no more time. It was Monday.

Maybe now, she could allow herself to think about the women she had met the day before. She was still afraid to let her thoughts stray there, but felt a strange curiosity. Iheoma had made a valid point, indeed the women were living testaments to it, and there must be countless others out there living under the same conditions as she had suddenly found herself. Some were aware, like the women she had met, while others were still ignorant or simply chose not to see the obvious. Had she been like one of those naïve women? She had long established that this was the case.

When Ada dropped Ego off at school, she could not help but wonder how many of the women doing the same thing were single. She was not comfortable with the thought of being a single mother. The concept seemed so foreign but surely, if she chose it, it would not be unbearable. Ada felt bad having this prejudice against single mothers. After all, Iheoma was an excellent mother who had never gotten married, and she was a good friend as well. But the way she chose to live her life was very non-conformist, an expression still unwelcome in their society.

When Ada got to her office, she was pleased to see that her assistant, Angela, had supervised the redecoration of the display room. The room was done up with wonderful furniture from Italy – a black leather cushioned sofa, stainless steel coffee table with a pristine glass top and white polar bear fur centre rug, giant Egyptian style flower pots with ostrich feathers, draped voile – giving an impression of faultless quality. It was a wonderful contrast to the gleaming dark marble tiles on the floor.

Sitting down behind her desk, Ada realized the irony of the services she provided and the cultural values she wanted so desperately to hold on to. She was selling modernity and globalisation through all the exotic pieces she used in her clients' houses. Most of her best pieces were imports from the West, from Europe and America. Yet while embracing the aesthetics of these places, she was not willing to adopt the parts of their culture that challenged that which she held dear as traditional African values. She still strongly believed that the concept of homosexuality was very much contrary to African culture. It was an import, like violent rap music, sophisticated armed robbery, nudity as fashion, and all such rubbish. Somehow, these negative imports had crept into her society and corrupted its very fabric. Like many Nigerians, she believed that homosexuality was a borrowed trait and not inherent in a person's biological make-up. And where else could an African learn such a thing?

The phone ringing jolted Ada from her reflections. She picked up the handset and gave the customary greeting, "Good morning, Concept Interiors, how can I help?"

Ada!" It was her cousin, Nkechi. "How are you?"

"I'm okay. Thank you for having Ego over the other day."

"Oh, it was nothing. I just wanted to know if you are okay."

"I'm okay. Just coming to terms with everything."

Silence.

It was a particular kind of silence. It was loaded with questions and curiosity and unspoken certainty. This was not the kind of silence that Ada was comfortable with.

"Have you made up your mind what you are going to

do?" Nkechi asked breaking the long pause.

"No. My choices are only limited to one of two things. Either I remain married or I don't."

"And…"

"And there is still the issue of my telling my parents and siblings, if I choose to tell them."

"But you have to tell them. The word is out. At least some people are already talking about it. You don't want them to hear this from the wrong sources."

"There will always be rumours. It will blow over after a short while, like all bad things said about people. I'm more concerned about the long term effects."

"I know what you mean," Nkechi said wearily.

"Do you really?"

"With you both having a child, I can understand that. Also dealing with the family, I can imagine the nightmare. If you both choose to separate, I also can see the dilemma in all that."

"Why can't it be simple?" Ada complained.

Why couldn't it indeed? Why did her decision seem to be tied to too many other fears? She certainly felt like she was damned if she did and damned if she didn't.

7

There was something markedly different when Adrian got to the office that Monday morning. He had had a deep sense of foreboding when he woke up and he could not quite place where all the negative energy was coming from. He had the upsetting feeling that there was something he ought to have done, something important, which he hadn't. He had racked his brain trying to figure out what it was, but kept hitting a blank wall. There was simply nothing he could imagine!

At the office, the feeling intensified. It had taken on a new face; it was more anxiety than any other thing. The almost hostile glare he received from many staff members was quite unsettling. Very few managed to mumble a pitiful "morning" and none offered eye contact.

Once within the confines of his private office, Adrian sighed in relief. He plugged in his laptop and tried to work but lacked concentration. The computer screen was a fuzzy blank glare, which seemed to hypnotize his senses, leaving him numb. His eyes remained open but he could see nothing, just white space. All he could register were the voices in his head that said repeatedly; 'They know what you are!' and he could not shake off a feeling of shame. He felt shame because he knew they were thinking he was sick, abnormal and surely a sinner already condemned to hell fire. He knew this was the average person's attitude towards people like him.

He shook his head in an attempt to clear his mind and keep focus. His vision adjusted to the blue screen of his computer and he noticed the writing there. He looked closely at the letters that appeared in bold print:

THEYKNOWWHATYOUARE
THEYKNOWWHATYOUARE...

Adrian jolted back in his seat in shock. He blinked his eyes several times and then stared at the screen of his computer again. It was blank now. No writing! He looked at his fingers as if to make sure that he had not in his subconscious typed the words, his fingers acting on their own will, not his. But no, his hands had not touched the keypad of his laptop. It was just a hallucination. He really was beginning to scare himself. His paranoia was increasing by the minute.

Just then, there was a slight knock on his door and before he could say anything, John Coker entered his office. Adrian stood up instinctively to greet him.

"Good morning, John." There was a hint of anxiety in his voice.

"Morning, Adrian," John replied in a very formal tone. "There's something important we have to discuss."

"There is?"

"Please have your seat," John pulled out one of the two leather chairs in front of Adrian's table and sat down.

Adrian lowered himself slowly into his seat, his eyes not leaving John for a second and his mind registering the stiffness in John's manner.

John began as soon as Adrian was seated. "I hate to be the one to bring this to you. But the management has advised me to talk to you about these things we have been hearing."

"What things, sir?" Adrian asked.

"There's a concern about your conduct as regards the recent fraud investigation and a possible complication," John said. "We are not saying you acted in a compromising fashion."

"I did not institute the investigation, sir," Adrian stressed. "Neither did I contribute to its outcome, but only provided verification of documents and evidence provided to me from the head office."

"I know…"

"And I don't believe this is the reason you are here," Adrian said hotly. "I believe you are here because of another matter and it would be less insulting to me if you admit it."

"No need to be rude, Mr. Njoko," John said sternly. "We don't want this leading into something nasty, but we have heard that one of the security men has alleged that you propositioned him inappropriately."

"What?" Adrian was shocked by this revelation. "That is ridiculous!"

"It may well be so. But I cannot deny that we have heard certain rumours about your sexual preferences in the last week."

Adrian felt his temple was going to explode. He could hear the heavy pounding of his heart and feel the hairs at the back of his neck stand.

"My personal life has nothing to do with my work," he said in a whisper. "Neither can the company suspend me or even fire me based on a perception of my sexual orientation. I know my rights."

"Nobody has said anything about suspension or dismissal," John said reassuringly. "All we are saying is that you take a break for a few days or even a few weeks if you so choose."

Adrian could not believe his ears. It sounded like a death sentence.

"I don't see any reason why I should take a break," he argued.

"It would be a paid leave," John offered.

"And if I refuse?"

"Then you put me in an awkward position. If we end up investigating the allegation, you may then be put on suspension and that will be bad for your record."

Silence.

Adrian recognized a threat when he heard one.

"All I'm asking is for you to take a short holiday. Let the tension here cool off and when you return things will be back in order. Think about it, okay?"

With that, John stood up and, after a momentary pause, turned round and exited, leaving Adrian to his thoughts and worries.

The whole episode was surreal to Adrian. He could not comprehend how anybody, not to talk of a security guard, would allege that he had propositioned him. And that his immediate bosses chose to believe such rubbish without conferring with him first surprised him. Was this because they believed the allegation or because they were afraid that he indeed might be gay? It was the latter and he knew it. Although under the company's staff handbook an individual could not be discriminated against due to his sexual orientation, Adrian knew that it would not hold in practice if you were anything other than heterosexual. Discrimination would come in various guises, such as being overlooked when it came to promotions or even verbal or physical abuse. This was one of the reasons he had wanted to be seen as the ideal professional with a sound family. And he had been, until recent events changed all that.

Adrian could also not understand how the company

could have stooped so low to start reacting to rumours such
as this absurd accusation! He could feel the nasty hands of
"Nigerianisation" tearing at the heart of what was once an
excellent multinational company with a sound American
approach to work. Nigerians so hated one another sometimes
that they would do anything to drag a successful person
down. Nigerians are like crabs in a bucket. Whenever one
seems to be rising above the others in an attempt to climb
out of the bucket, other crabs claw at it and eventually pull
it down. This vicious cycle kept repeating itself time after
time.

It dawned on Adrian when he reconsidered the full
implication that the guard's allegation was one of sexual
harassment. But the truth was he, Adrian, was being
harassed because of his perceived sexuality, and the legal
system in the country was not equipped to deal with
anything remotely resembling this and Adrian knew that
even if there was a law against any such thing it was not
meant to favour homosexuals. In fact, there was a law
against homosexuality! He vividly remembered reading
on the front cover of a Sunday newspaper some years back
about how a homosexual couple was paraded naked. The
story had a lewd headline and detailed how the couple had
been hounded by their curious neighbours who did not
understand what kind of relationship the two men shared,
and how they had broken into their two-room apartment
one night to catch the men in bed together. They were
beaten out of their flat and marched to the nearby police
station, stark naked. What many did not know was that the
police in turn had forced the men to simulate sexual acts
while a photographer took pictures that were sold to the
newspapers.

Adrian remembered how horrified he felt as he read
the story. He had thought about his old friend, Abdul, and

his lover. This could easily have been both of them! It was scary no one had questioned the neighbours for breaking and entering someone else's apartment. No one had talked about the invasion of privacy and fundamental human rights abuse committed against the men. No one cared. And no one even bothered to ask where these men were after the newspaper exposé, but Adrian could only guess; they probably had been forgotten in some tiny, smelly, rotten cell inhabited by a dozen or so inmates waiting for a trial that may never come, with no hope of family ever stepping forward to bail them out lest they too should be condemned.

Adrian had silently thanked his stars that he was married and living a heterosexual life. He knew he would never have survived an event like that. The humiliation would have been too much to bear. That experience was one of the most dreaded realities of every gay man he knew; to be caught in the act or even accused of being gay and then paraded like a freak after a life sentence of shame.

He pondered if he should call John's bluff and resist taking leave, but another part of his mind warned of the danger of putting the power of the corporate body to the test. The final answer was a hushed sigh in his ear telling him that he would never win a fight like this. People like John would shred every respectable impression other people had of him and, afterwards, would literally parade him in all his nakedness and vulnerability to be laughed at and condemned.

A cold shiver surged through his body. He knew what it was. It was an old familiar foe. Fear!

Adrian decided he needed the break after all. He needed to use the free time to work things out with his wife and family. Once he had convinced himself about this, Adrian pulled out a leave form from his desk and filled it out for a two-week holiday. During his lunch break, he submitted the form himself to John's office. He didn't wait around for small talk, but stayed long enough for John to sign the paperwork and offer a conciliatory smile.

Rather than leave immediately, Adrian stayed till the official closing time. He was not going to feed the rumour mill in the office, knowing that a lot would be speculated if people saw him leaving early. But more importantly, he did not want to endure the suffocating weight of the people's contempt, of which he had had a brief taste that morning. So he was among the last to leave that evening and to his surprise, the security men at the gate were all there. They all avoided his gaze and he, in return, did not utter a word to any one of them.

A sudden rapping on the passenger's window startled Adrian. It was Rotimi bent over so that their eyes met. Adrian brought the glass down with the remote switch.

"Good evening, sir."

"Rotimi, how are you?"

"I'm fine, sir. Can I get a lift, sir?"

"Sure."

Rotimi slid into the front seat of the passenger side. As he adjusted the seatbelt, Adrian set the car in motion and drove off.

"So, where are you off to?" he asked jovially.

"Anywhere you are going to, sir. I just thought I should spend some time in your company, sir."

"Enough of this sir nonsense, Rotimi," Adrian laughed. "Is it so difficult to simply say my name? Just call me Adrian."

Rotimi persisted. "You are my boss, sir. I have to show my respect."

Adrian decided not to push it. He could see Rotimi was beginning to squirm uncomfortably in his seat, and Adrian didn't want him to feel that way. In fact, he was impressed with Rotimi for disregarding whatever people might think of him by still showing support for Adrian. Rotimi's waiting in the car park for him was a brave show of solidarity.

"I'm starting my leave tomorrow," Adrian said out loud.

"Really, sir?" Rotimi said after a short pause. "I hope they are not making you leave!"

"I just need a short holiday. Nobody is making me leave, okay?"

"Okay, sir."

Adrian glanced at him. He was unusually quiet. Normally he was a chatterbox but now he sat quietly in his corner with no move to contribute any information. There was a serene look on his face that Adrian had not seen before.

"Hey!" Adrian suddenly said. "What's the latest gossip in the office? I am surprised you haven't told me what story is making the rounds now."

It was obvious Rotimi was struggling to speak. His eyebrows creased as he thought of the best way to phrase his words. Adrian also noticed a nervous tick by the corner of the left side of his mouth.

"Well," Rotimi began slowly, "there's talk that Boniface, the security man, says you…"

"Yes, I heard.It's all rubbish, you know that, don't you?"

"I know," Rotimi said solemnly.

The car came to a halt. There was a long queue of cars from both sides of the road stuck in the rush-hour go-slow; even the service lanes had been taken over by desperate cars, and a flood of commercial bike riders, okadas, fought with them for space on the road. It was a noisy bottleneck. Horns were blaring and the heat outside was unbearable. Adrian was thankful for his car's air conditioning.

"Sir," Rotimi said, "I like women. A lot."

Adrian remained quiet. There was nothing really he could say in reply to that disclosure.

"But," Rotimi continued, "I have been with a man before."

He stopped to look defensively at Adrian, waiting for a reaction. Negative. Positive. Any reaction. But Adrian's expression remained passive and unflinching.

"I have this friend who works in the bank," Rotimi continued, after gauging that he was not being judged. "He is gay. He's a very nice person. It happened one night with him. I don't know why we did it, but whatever!"

Rotimi lifted his shoulder in a shrug. He stole a peek at Adrian again. Adrian had just moved the car about a yard since they ran into the traffic. His facial expression was still unreadable.

"But I'm not gay," Rotimi stressed. "Although I have had some guys step up to me sometimes. It doesn't really bother me. It's almost flattering."

A long silence ensued, broken only when Adrian moved the car another inch or so and was forced to horn in warning at an okada rider who veered dangerously close to his car.

"Rotimi," Adrian finally replied, "thank you for telling me this. But there is something you must know about me."

Rotimi waited anxiously. He had turned to face Adrian fully but their eyes could not meet as Adrian stared straight ahead, his eyes locked on the car in front of him.

"I'm not like you. I am gay."

"It doesn't matter, sir," Rotimi said reassuringly.

"It matters a lot. But you have to know that my sexuality has never interfered with my work or my family."

Rotimi was quiet.

"Did you ever suspect?"

Rotimi shook his head. "No."

Adrian tilted his head so his eyes finally met with

Rotimi.'s A silent understanding passed between the two men in the stillness of the car. It was a pact with a promise of secrecy and confidentiality: you know my secret, now you must keep it safe and locked up so no one else can use it to hurt me!

The moment passed. Traffic eased up a bit and Adrian was able to get to the first intersection that turned off to Ozumba Mbadiwe Road. 1004 loomed ahead, a giant edifice shooting out in the sky like a colossal sore thumb in the midst of newer and better buildings.

As Adrian slowly made his way in the traffic, he allowed his mind to begin to process Rotimi's revelation. Surprising as it was, he was not the least shocked. There were many men like Rotimi out there, 'undercover brothers,' self-proclaimed women lovers, who, when the opportunity arose, would go with men as well. Someone once told Adrian that all men had the tendency to turn out gay; it was intrinsic to their nature. This was why many men were violent homophobes, driven by the fear that at their weakest, they too may succumb to their inherent nature. Adrian wondered how many of these men were out there. Was it possible that a higher percentage of Nigerian men were undercover brothers than not?

He knew he could not judge Rotimi, neither could he criticize him. After all, he had married a woman despite his love for men. Who was the bigger sinner? Who was lying to himself the more?

"Where are we going?" Rotimi asked in confusion, noticing the car was approaching the gate that led to the 1004 apartments.

"1004," Adrian said. "My wife found out about me. I've been staying here for the last couple of days."

"Wow!" Rotimi mouthed. "Will you be getting a divorce?"

Adrian did not reply for a moment. "I don't know, I've just been taking it one day at a time."

"Is that why you are taking a leave?"

"Kind of," Adrian simply said.

When they got to Abdul's empty apartment Adrian began to feel slight discomfort from how close Rotimi was keeping to his side. He had first noticed as they entered the elevator, when Rotimi had deliberately moved closer to him even though there was lots of space around them. Even now, as Adrian made to go to the bedroom to change from his office wear, he could sense a raw and anxious energy directly behind him, a very intense presence. He turned around swiftly and almost bumped lip-to-lip into Rotimi. They were so close that he could feel Rotimi's warm breath on his face. It smelt of stale peppermints. Time stood still as they stared at each other. Adrian tried responding to the smile Rotimi was giving him but his upper lip only managed to quiver nervously.

Slowly, Rotimi began leaning towards Adrian. At the point when their lips almost touched, Adrian backed away, breaking the spell.

"Rotimi stop! You don't have to do this."

"I want to, Adrian."

"No, you don't!" Adrian pressed. "You only think you do just to show me that you are there for me and I appreciate this but you know I can't let this happen."

Rotimi looked down and turned away slowly. Adrian watched him and thought he could sense relief emanating from him.

"I think you should go now, Rotimi," Adrian insisted, "and thank you."

"Yes, sir."

Rotimi dragged himself to the door in a slow disconsolate shuffle, not turning round to look at Adrian until he got to the entrance. He gave one last smile, but it wasn't from his heart, just a mere lifting of cheeks that did not reflect in defeated eyes. He waved in mock salute at Adrian before he stepped outside and shut the door behind him.

Adrian closed his eyes as he collapsed on the sofa. His heart was beating fiercely against his chest, threatening to burst through his ribcage. He sat up and held his head in his hands as he thought about what almost happened. It was a close shave! He could not deny that he was for a moment strongly attracted to Rotimi, but it was not an emotional connection he felt, only sexual. This was what scared him, this strong sexual pull. He was glad he had made Rotimi leave or else he would not have had the will power to prevent the inevitable.

But he was left wondering: are gay men sexually attracted to all men simply because they are men? Are heterosexual men sexually attracted to any woman simply because she is a woman?

As he lit a fresh cigarette, he could not but notice how much his hands trembled.

◎ ◎ ◎

YOU ARE such a fool Rotimi. A big, big fool; that is what you are.

Thus Rotimi cursed himself as he made his way out of the apartment complex. He found himself taking the stairs instead of the elevator. Hearing the thud of his footsteps was vaguely soothing and the long minutes this solitary walk afforded him were exactly what he needed. He could not erase from his head the look in Adrian's eyes as Adrian had stopped him. There was a deep humanity in those eyes that had shocked his very soul – an understanding and gratitude that Rotimi felt he did not deserve. Adrian had said that Rotimi was only drawn to him because he felt he needed to show an affinity with him, but that was not entirely true. Rotimi was drawn to Adrian for no explicable reason. Adrian was a good man; he had been nothing but good to Rotimi. His eyes, his eyes... Adrian's eyes.

Many years before now, Rotimi had been acquainted with similar eyes. They belonged to another young boy, Ella. Ella had been one of those very unfortunate boys who joined boarding school a term late and midway into the new term. He had been transferred from another secondary school and that was all anyone knew about him. There had been a lot of hush-hush about Ella. All that people remembered was he had a very attractive mother who spoke funny, and later it was discovered that she was not Nigerian, but Jamaican. His father was never seen or spoken of. From the first day Ella stepped into Federal Government College Ugwolawo, he kept to himself. No one ever saw him taking his bath in the morning before the wake-up bell went off, and he barely ever ate his food in the dining hall. He had no close friend nor was he ready to join any clique. He was a strange one.

There were two distinguishing things about Ella – his eyes and his hair. His irises were a dull hazel hue and he had thick, curly, cropped hair. The students thought he was what they called a half-caste because he had a foreign mother, but the thing was that both his parents were black. Ella himself was as dark as a Mandingo warrior, burnt black by the hot West African sun like most of the other children. Lacking any useful information about Ella, and with his unwillingness to socialise with the other students, countless variations of his strangeness circulated round the school. There was talk that he relaxed his hair like the girls, but no one had seen him do this, and that his eyes were that colour because he was almost an albino. How that was feasible based on his skin tone, no one cared to explain! Rotimi and his clique of friends had had their fun too, jeering at the timid Ella whenever they walked past him in the classroom corridors, in front of everyone including the girls. They would line up in a straight line and then proceed to mimic the way he walked, intentionally exaggerating his ethereal gait.

It didn't help that Ella was soft-spoken and prone to crying when mocked excessively, and Rotimi and his friends found no end to the laughter they drew when they made nonsense of the strange-looking black boy with the light eyes and curly hair.

One night during prep Rotimi had sneaked off a full hour before it ended to meet up with Cecilia Ayeni. Rotimi had had his eyes on Cecilia throughout the term and felt lucky that she had agreed to meet him by the footpath junction that linked the girls' hostel to staff quarters. The junction was popularly known as 'Lovers' Lane' because the trees that criss-crossed the path created a discreet meeting point where the senior boys usually rendezvoused with girls. When Rotimi got to Lovers' Lane, Cecilia was already there waiting. She was not the only one though; she had her usual tail, the Dehinde twins, Molara and Molade, who followed her everywhere, just a few feet away.

Rotimi didn't know what to do at Lovers' Lane. He had never met a girl before under such circumstances. He had heard tales that some of the boys who came to this spot were actually very prepared and had sex under the trees, hidden away from peering eyes. He had only heard this, but not met anybody who had done the act itself. The thought of sex and the possibility that that night may be his initiation made the sleeping appendage between his legs awaken. Rotimi, who had the terrible habit of not wearing underwear, felt ashamed then and wished he had worn a pair that night as his shorts protruded at an odd angle. He stuck his hands into pocket and stylishly grabbed his penis to shield its protrusion from Cecilia. He was not sure if she had noticed it, but he could see that she was smiling. Without saying anything she rushed to him and placed unsteady, slurry lips on his before scuffling away with her friends in tow. He heard their girly giggles as they disappeared towards the female hostel.

Excited, and with a throbbing phallus, Rotimi had run off as well to his hostel. He knew that everyone was still in the classrooms and if the house captain or any of the real seniors – the final year seniors – were to catch him in the hostel at that hour, he would be in trouble. But Cecilia had just kissed him. His first real kiss. He could still smell the vanilla of her lotion and he could not erase the image of adults coupling from his head. During the holiday he had watched a blue movie with an older cousin of his and had been very aroused by what he saw, and he imagined that the next time he met Cecilia at Lover's Lane, he might do some of the things from the movie.

But next time was too long a time to wait. He made his way to the bathroom stall of the hostel, knowing that the doors to the rooms were locked during prep while the bathrooms were always open. He went into one of the ironing rooms that overlooked the showers. His excitement was great, so was the pain in his groin. He dropped his pants and looked briefly at the turgid weight that nodded at him. He closed his eyes and slowly began to stroke himself, his senses responding to the residual memory of Cecilia's lips and smell.

How well he remembered that day even now. As he opened his eyes after ejaculating, Ella stood inches away staring at him, his gaze fixed on Rotimi's now-deflated penis. Rotimi grew very hot in the face with embarrassment which quickly turned to pure anger.

"What are you looking at, you faggot?" Rotimi screamed at him. "You fucking homo!"

Ella had looked into his eyes then, very much the same way Adrian had just done, before saying, "Rotimi stop!"

Rotimi remembered pushing Ella aside and rushing away. Later he would tell his friends that Ella had snuck up on him that night and tried to touch his penis. They all laughed and found yet another insult to add to their repertoire for dainty Ella. Then, a couple of nights after that incident, they ganged up and waylaid Ella as he returned from prep. As they punched and kicked him, calling him "faggot", "obirin" and "homo", Ella had kept still, his swelling eyes fixed on Rotimi's.

Rotimi still felt enormous guilt about that incident. He never had a chance to apologise to Ella and once they finished secondary school he never saw him again. They never became friends and he never knew if Ella was indeed a homosexual. He had wondered for a long time how a boy could stand and watch another in such a private and personal moment. What could Ella have been thinking? Why had he stayed and watched? And why, through the humiliation he faced for his remaining years at Ugwolawo, had he never told anyone the truth of that night, revealing to all what Rotimi was doing to himself? Ella could have talked and shamed him and the tables would have turned and it would have been Rotimi to spend the better part of secondary school in disgrace.

If Adrian hadn't stopped him, he would have kissed him. He did not know why he was drawn to Adrian that way; it certainly wasn't like the time with his friend, Debo, the banker. With Debo he had been a little giddy after lots of alcohol and fooling around in a club, and had always had his suspicions about Debo's sexuality. But there was a weakness in Rotimi that anyone, man or woman, could easily manipulate, and that was his vanity. Rotimi could not resist it when people complimented his good looks. Men hardly did so, but when women met him they often could not help but comment on his eyes, his slender nose, his lips or broad shoulders. So when Debo started teasing him and pouring suggestive compliments his way, Rotimi had no control over what happened next, he only knew his ego was engorged, like another part of his anatomy. They did it and Rotimi had felt terrible afterwards. He left Debo's house the next day and they both never spoke about the incident again.

The difference with Adrian just now was that Rotimi was very sober and was not influenced by ego. Thank God Adrian stopped him. What did it mean that he almost kissed another man out of his own volition? Did this make him gay? He did not feel gay. He had never considered himself a homosexual all his life. He certainly would not rush out and look for a man to sleep with tomorrow or the day after, no. He was not gay, yet he would have kissed another man. He would have kissed Adrian.

◉ ◉ ◉

IT WAS a boisterous evening at Abdul's apartment.

George was in town. George, like Adrian, had given up his traditional name, Effiong. Necessity had made him change his identity. Unlike Adrian who had been baptised as such, and had the name on relevant documents, George had simply invented his English name and sworn an affidavit in court. All this he did before he finally relocated to Germany with his German partner, Johan.

They had met while George worked as cabin crew

for Lufthansa. Johan had no chance the minute George approached him in the business class cabin and offered him a drink with a dazzling smile. He was hooked. They started seeing each other shortly after that and within a year, Johan persuaded George to come and live with him in Düsseldorf; not that George needed much persuasion anyway. George had always hated Nigeria. According to him, "Nigeria was not ready for the likes of him yet." On one of his trips to Germany, he had secretly held a gay wedding with Johan. It was nothing fancy, just signing of papers and exchange of rings with two witnesses, Johan's parents. When George returned to Nigeria from that trip he did not tell his family he was now married, only a few of his gay friends knew. Some were shocked at how brave he was; others simply scorned him out of jealousy, but George didn't care. After three months, when his immigration papers were ready, he simply informed his family that he was relocating to Germany to work. That was ten years back and this was his first visit to Nigeria since he left the country. He had returned to attend his mother's funeral.

Adrian was impressed with how stunning George still looked. He was trim and fit with no sign of body fat. One could tell he spent hours daily on the treadmill. True to his fashion, when he breezed in that evening, it was with much fanfare and grace. George was wearing black leather skintight trousers that left everyone wondering how he managed to pull it off in the sweltering heat. He complemented his trousers with a low-cut T-shirt and ankle high boots. A true picture to behold!

While George and Femi were in one of the bedrooms playing catch-up, Adrian and Abdul remained in the living room. Adrian had earlier told Abdul over the phone about his forced leave and the episode with Rotimi, and this was the only chance they had to really talk about it.

"You cannot accept to be bullied like this. I'm sorry but I believe you are being discriminated against at your workplace. I know a good lawyer you can talk to."

"It's okay. I don't mind it just this one time."

"It's not okay!" Abdul stressed. "If you allow this to happen this one time, you automatically give them the right to do it again and again."

"I meant I really do need some time off now. I have to sort out things with Ada. I need to still see my brothers and patch things up with them and my parents…"

Abdul studied Adrian briefly. He kept his eyes trained on Adrian's for a full minute before he looked away and sighed.

"Now tell me again about this Rotimi issue," Abdul finally asked.

Adrian sighed and lifted his shoulders in a questioning gesture.

Rhetorically he asked, "can I say he came on to me? He admitted he had been with a man before and then tried to kiss me."

"Be careful with that one," Abdul advised. "He seems to be confused about who he is."

"Interesting you should say that. I felt the same way too. Like he was pushing himself to do it. It was like a pity thing. I just felt he thought he needed to show me that he does not disapprove of me."

"Still be careful," Abdul warned. "Even if later you find yourself attracted to him, you can't do anything with him. No matter how it is viewed, he is your subordinate at work and there's already talk of your trying to take advantage of another one."

Adrian knew what Abdul was saying was true especially when he remembered how aroused he had felt when Rotimi tried to kiss him, but all the same he resented Abdul for stressing his warning. It was almost as if Abdul had somehow read his mind and guaged his interest.

Just then, there was a burst of noise as both George and Femi exited the bedroom. George was laughing loudly and holding his sides while Femi was practically rolling on the floor beside him.

"Bitte mal!" George cried out in German. "Was gibt? What's with the long faces?"

"We are fine," Abdul said, smiling as he passed a fleeting gaze towards Femi. "You never did say what you've done to that man of yours."

George sighed.

"He wanted to stay in the hotel." He rolled his eyes. "All the better for me. Sometimes him wahala tire me."

"What!" Abdul exclaimed. "Is that frustration I detect in your voice? A whole diva like you!"

"Stop making fun of me," George said in mock annoyance. "But sometimes I feel so frustrated with Johan. He wants me to be a certain way to please his false sense of accomplishment. I have had to put up with the cold of Europe, learn the awful language and make countless sacrifices."

"It's the path you chose. You complained just as much when you lived here."

George admitted. "It's so hard sometimes. No matter what I do, I will never be an equal in Germany. There are still places I can't go with Johan or we may be attacked. What annoys me most is when Johan fails to see how much sacrifice I make for him."

"But you look great," Abdul said. "You can't complain that Johan is not looking after you."

"Please!" George sighed. "I have a job. In fact, I work in Prada, so I make my own money."

"So he doesn't support you!"

"I didn't say he doesn't. We have a lovely house which he paid for and cars and all the stuff I'd always dreamed of," George added a bit defensively.

"And!"

"And I miss home badly. I miss you guys, my friends. My family. The madness of Nigeria! I miss it all."

"We missed you too," Femi chipped in.

"I was just telling Femi how much prejudice and racism I still have to face in Europe. It's amazing that no matter how established an African man is, he remains a second-class citizen. I carry an EU passport now but I'm still detained by immigration when I travel."

"What has Johan to do with any of this?" Abdul asked.

"He has become boring. His age is catching up with him. He's fifteen years older than I am. His body is sagging out and he's not as adventurous as he used to be, nor is he as fabulous as I am. I need a real man, you know."

Femi joined him in laughing but both Adrian and Abdul exchanged worried looks.

"You shouldn't talk like that you know. When you do that you live up to the stereotype many people have of the gay man," Abdul admonished.

"How so?" George challenged.

"You sound like you only used Johan to check out of this country and gain a new nationality."

"He used me too, you know. I was his one chance of getting a fabulous partner. I became his trophy spouse. All his friends were simply jealous."

There was more laughter from both Femi and George.

"If you are so unhappy with Johan, why not tell him! Why not tell him and return home?"

"Home being Nigeria?" George said. "God forbid! This country hasn't changed... No, it has, it is worse than when I left ten years ago. The government is still corrupt, nothing works and there's still so much poverty here. What is there to come back to?"

"But you just talked about how much you missed here!"

"Yes, I do miss this country when I'm abroad, but truthfully, it's the idea of what I expect the country to be I miss the most. I keep dreaming that when I come home, everything will be all right. We'll have a good government and a workable democracy where the people's voice actually does matter. I imagine tarred roads, streetlights, good hospitals, constant electricity, religious tolerance and a sense of equality despite sexual orientation or sex for that matter. When I dream and see the country like this, I do miss it."

"If you come home, you could be among those trying to change the country to a better place" Abdul said. "You can come make a difference, you know!"

"Yeah, right!" George laughed. "What chance does someone like me have? A fag, homo, teebee!" George recited the common derogatory terms for gay people.

"You are impossible!" Abdul sighed fondly.

Later that night, while Adrian lay in bed alone, he thought about George and the life he chose for himself, and also all the things he had said about missing Nigeria. He had so many great expectations! He also had Johan with whom he no longer was in love, and a whole new nationality. Were people like George heroes like many gay people imagined; men who damned all and followed their heart even if it led them to Europe and to marry the men they loved? Or were they actually cowards and opportunists, taking advantage of foreigners to escape to a make-believe paradise?

8

It had been raining a lot. A senseless sort of rain whose rhythm and cycle could not be predicted. One minute it would be hard, the next moment a light drizzle. The rain could decide to flow down from the left and the next minute switch to the right, or even intermingle with no set pattern. What made it unbearable was that there was no functional drainage in the city and so the gutters overflowed with brown muddy water filled with the rubbish of the past weeks – paper, rubber bags, banana peels, shrubs, waste. Lagos became a clogged-up island of filthy water. Even the so-called upmarket part of town would flood, water collecting in the potholes that littered the streets and overflowing the gutters. In some parts of Lagos, the water level would rise to above twelve inches and find its way into many houses. Then there was the NEPA issue. Whenever there was the slightest sign of rain, the electricity would go off, leaving in its wake a depression that surpassed the darkness.

It was in such rain and darkness that Ada received her unexpected visitor. She had just instructed Isioma to switch on the generator when the doorbell rang. Isioma had grabbed an umbrella and dashed out into the rain and had soon returned with a woman who had two military escorts holding up huge umbrellas to shield her from the downpour. Ada quickly recognized the visitor as Carol Obosi.

"Wait for me in the car," Carol instructed the two military escorts. "I will call you when I'm ready to leave."

She turned round, shot Ada a wide smile and breezed into the living room. Ada couldn't help but imagine her as a butterfly still. She was wearing a flowing, multicoloured chiffon boubou wrapped around her body. Her hair, done up in thick braids, was piled high on her head and bound together with a chiffon wrap made from the same fabric as her dress.

"Ada! I just dropped by to say hello."

"Carol!"

"What can we do about this bloody rain? It's like a river has taken over the island."

Carol dropped herself on the sofa and carefully placed her handbag on the coffee table in front of her. Ada joined her on an adjacent easy chair.

"Carol, what a pleasant surprise!" Ada finally said. It was not, and Ada hoped her voice did not convey this fact.

"I usually don't like dropping in on people like this, but since I was in your neighbourhood and the rain… I decided to drop by anyway."

Just then they both heard the soft purring of the generator coming from outside and, seconds later, the lights were back on. Ada picked up the remote control on the coffee table and switched on the air conditioner that hung on one of the walls. Carol sighed in relief.

"Thank God for generators!"

Ada just kept watching her. She didn't know what to make of this meeting. It was the very first time Carol had paid her a visit in her home, and Ada wasn't quite sure if she welcomed it at all. She was still getting over the shock of the last time they had met and the dreadful feeling of being initiated into a secret cult of women married to gay men. Having Carol in her house did not help the feeling whatsoever.

Carol leaned over and dived into her bag, whipping out a cigarette and was about to light it when she noticed the stern look in Ada's eyes. She quickly replaced the cigarette and lighter.

"Can we talk candidly?"

Ada shrugged indifferently.

"Is your husband in? What about your daughter?"

"My husband is not here and it's okay to talk, my daughter is in her room."

Carol shrugged and pushed herself snugly back on the sofa so she could be more relaxed and comfortable.

"When you left my house last Sunday, I noticed how uneasy you felt about what we told you."

Ada continued to hold her stare.

"Maybe opening up to you the way we did was not the best approach. I understand how shocking it must have all been. But letting you know the truth is the only way to help you get over this quickly.

"I wasn't always this cynical. I wasn't always this strong. The time I was first faced with Major's homosexuality, I was devastated and crushed. I was also very angry. I could not understand why he would do such a thing to me. I kept blaming myself for it. It was as if I was rubbish in bed, so useless that I drove him into the arms of a man. I threatened to leave him so many times, but I could not bring myself to reveal the reason why to anyone. I healed with time. I made up my mind to stay with him. After all, a marriage is always about being there in good times and bad times, in sickness and in health. Granted, my situation was more bad times than anything. I felt so isolated. I felt like I was the only woman this had ever happened to, but soon I started meeting other women with similar problems. I soon realized that there was a whole world of us with the same issues. Knowing and meeting some of these women has made me stronger. I don't feel so angry any more. I can almost understand why Major lied to me. In his way, he loves me and if he had told me before we married, I certainly would not have stayed with him or married him. His fear of losing me kept him silent and that, to me, was his way of showing me he loved me. He did not want to lose me."

Silence followed. Ada tried to say something reasonable like "Thank you!" or "I understand and agree with you," but she could not.

"Should I get you something to drink?"

The statement clearly threw Carol off balance. Her face registered confusion and then she shook her head slightly and smiled knowingly.

"I'm just fine, thank you."

Silence.

The silence was driving Ada mad. The silence exposed their difference as women. The silence judged them both, mocked them even. It threatened to speak of their vulnerability. The silence refused to remain silent.

"Carol," Ada finally broke the stillness, "I know what you are trying to say and I appreciate your concern. Some matters are private and should be dealt as such. I don't know how to share my pain with anybody other than myself. Contrary to what you think, I'm moving on already."

"You are?" Carol said. "I know you don't like me, so whatever I say to you will have no meaning."

"I don't dislike you, Carol."

"I see the way you look at me when you think I'm not watching."

"I don't hate you. I do disapprove of certain habits of yours, like smoking..."

"And my flamboyant lifestyle," Carol interrupted her, "and I'm sure you disapprove of my choice to remain with my husband despite knowing he sleeps with men."

"We are very different people, Carol. We make different choices for good or bad. If the choices we make are the wrong ones, we learn from them and try to avoid repeating the mistakes."

"That is true," Carol agreed. "That is so true."

Later that night, after Carol had gone and the rain had stopped, Ada wondered who was more in denial. That Carol actually believed that her husband loved her and had married her for this reason, was incomprehensible to Ada. But Ada could identify with the shame of having to face her people and tell them she would be leaving her husband. What excuse would she give to them to justify her leaving? How would she shame the man she had lived with for so many years and called husband? Certainly his shame would be her shame to carry as well! People would ask, "How come you didn't know?" And what would she say then? What answers would she give?

◎ ◎ ◎

"MUMMY, WHERE is daddy?"

Ada had just returned from office. She was in her bedroom trying to change and Ego was standing by her door dragging a black doll by its hand. There were traces of tears in Ego's eyes and Ada noticed she was holding back more.

"Mummy, why doesn't daddy come home any more?"

Ada sighed gently. She pulled the jacket she was wearing and in its place put on a sleeveless T-shirt. It had been a busy day at the office and what she wanted was a peaceful evening, not a whining child.

"You speak with daddy every day."

"Why can't I see daddy every day?" Ego persisted. "Why doesn't daddy sleep here any more?"

Ada rolled her eyes. She couldn't deal with this at the

moment. She had only that morning hinted to her brother, Uche, that she might be leaving Adrian, and the calls had not stopped since then. Her brother had pried and quizzed her on her decision but she had not given him anything concrete. "This is not a suitable telephone conversation," she had simply replied to his further questioning. Then her father called. His timbre voice still scared her. He demanded to know what was going on.

"Is he maltreating you? Did he lift his hands on you… tell me and I will have him sorted out."

"No, dad," she said, "Adrian never lifted a finger on me."

"Then what is this rubbish about a separation? Is he having an affair with another woman?"

"No, dad."

"Then what is it? If he is not beating you and he is not with another woman, why do you want to desert your marital home?"

"Dad, it's not what you think. This is between Adrian and me," she said weakly. She felt herself crumbling under his interrogation.

"Is the problem you?"

"What? How?"

"Are you cheating on him?"

"No, no, no… Daddy why would you think that?"

"I don't see what would warrant a married couple to separate other than the reasons I gave, and even all those can be resolved with the aid of family. Now, if your husband is good to you and not cheating on you and you still want to leave him then maybe the problem is with you and not him."

"Things are not always that simple, dad," she countered. "It's not always as simple as you think."

"Then tell me what the problem is."

"I will when I can. I promise."

The episode was quite uncomfortable for Ada and she was glad when, eventually, her father hung up. Now, how would she begin to address her daughter's query? She had at least tried by letting Adrian speak to Ego on the phone daily, as she couldn't even lie to her that her father had travelled. If she had, Ego would have been quick to point out to her that "Daddy always calls every day when he travels."

"I want my daddy!" Ego suddenly screamed. The shrill that followed was deafening and Ada had to cover her ears with her hands.

"Stop that!" Ada yelled back at her. "Stop it!"

"I want daddy!" Ego cried in a smaller voice.

"So do I, Ego," Ada joined her.

Isioma rushed up at that moment. She motioned to carry Ego away and Ada nodded her consent. Ego's wailing increased as she left, screaming "Daddy, daddy, daddy…" but Ada closed her eyes and heart to the cry. She could not deal with the pain any more.

◉ ◉ ◉

"SHE JUST keeps crying every day," Ada sighed.

She was having tea with Nkechi in her office. Nkechi had called earlier to say she would be coming over just before lunch and Ada had begged her to come earlier if possible.

Nkechi sat across from her in the little showroom Ada used to entertain her more important clients. It was a well-furnished room with some of Ada's best pieces from Europe. Beside the teapot was a stack of glossy magazines; all dealt with homes and gardens.

"I've tried everything, Nkechi," Ada said, "but she keeps crying for him. I even let them talk for over thirty minutes yesterday on the phone and she still cried when I had to end the call. It's driving me crazy."

"She's only a child, Ada. Give her some time to make the necessary adjustments. She can't understand right now."

"I think she loves him more than she loves me."

"She's only a child, Ada."

"What if she loves him more? She would only end up hating me more for keeping them apart."

Nkechi sighed and took a sip from her cup.

"You are not the only one whose child hates her."

"What are you talking about?"

"I didn't tell you this before," Nkechi began inertly. "The last time Ego was at my place, I ended up smacking Junior. I slapped him pretty hard actually."

"Why?" Ada asked. "What did he do?"

Nkechi closed her eyes as she tried to compose her words. Her eyebrows knotted and there was a crease on her forehead.

"Ada, have you noticed how Junior is always quiet?"

"Yes."

"How he never wants to play with the other boys!"

"Yes."

"How he never seems to want to play with his toys!"

"Yes… where is all this leading to?"

"Has it ever struck you how effeminate my Junior is?"

Silence. It was a thoughtful kind, the kind that was quickly followed by a remarkable awareness.

"I hit him because I was afraid. I think Junior may be gay!"

"What?" Ada gasped. "Why would you think that?"

"Didn't you hear the word I said?" Nkechi asked. "All the signs are there. As a parent it is my duty to notice and correct it before it is too late. I can't encourage him to continue with his girlish ways."

"And what has Obi got to say about all this?"

"He wouldn't listen to me. He said I should never ever hit his son again. His son! Can you imagine?"

"Nkechi, he is just a child! He doesn't know anything about sex or sexual orientations."

"Adrian was a child at a point in his life. Maybe if someone had corrected his behaviour earlier, he would never have turned out gay."

"How do you know that for sure? How do you know that he was not born that way and nothing could have changed him?"

Nkechi looked at her funnily with an expression that seemed to say, "where is all this rubbish talk coming from?"

"Anyway, as I was saying," Nkechi pressed on, "Junior has stopped speaking to me ever since that day. He manages to muster 'good morning, mummy' 'good afternoon, mummy' 'goodnight, mummy' and that's all. He avoids me like I have the plague. I don't know what to do. He simply hates me now."

"He doesn't hate you," Ada assured her. "He's just afraid of you."

"I hope so! But what will I do if my son turns out to be gay?" Nkechi sighed.

Ada did not know the answer to that. She could only picture the sweet little boy, Junior. He was such a lovely little child who smiled a lot and was always shying away from adults. He did enjoy playing with his little sister and cousin and there was an element of the feminine in him, but that surely said nothing of his sexuality! But if Nkechi's fear was justified and some day Junior was to announce to his family that he was gay, would that change the deep feeling of love she had for him? Would she love him less? Would Nkechi love him less?

"I will always love my son no matter what!" Nkechi

said defiantly as if she had been reading Ada's mind.

"And so you should," Ada said before realizing what it meant.

She could not advocate that Nkechi love her son any less because he was showing effeminate traits that may or may not point to his future sexual orientation. But in feeling this way, she quite clearly saw the incongruity of her own situation. Should she love Adrian any less because he was gay?

But this was certainly a different case, wasn't it? She pondered. Junior was an innocent little child. Adrian was a grown man. And he had deliberately deceived her. She was angry with him for this, but she could not determine if this was the main reason. She feared to dig any deeper for the real reason, lest she should find her contempt and disgust of having to be a victim of his deception. Or was there more to it? Or was it simply because he was...

She focused back on Nkechi's face and for the first time saw a different picture from the clear beauty she had always known. Now there were lines on her forehead, worry lines. There were also traces of crow's feet by the corner of her eyes. Ada noticed a silver string of gray hair tucked away discreetly inside the fold of Nkechi's hair. It was clear this issue was clearly weighing on Nkechi's mind. A mother's worry! It made Ada think about Adrian's mother. Had she at any time while Adrian was growing up worried about his sexuality? Had she maybe known that her son was different from other boys? Was that why there was a deep sense of relief when he brought her home to be presented as a bride? She had sensed the relief even then but had brushed it aside as mere expectations.

"My dear," Nkechi sighed, "it's not easy being a mother. It seems like we have to worry about every other thing."

"True."

"Not only are we mothers to our children but also to our husbands as well," Nkechi added with a roll of her eyes. "Everyone blames the mother when a child turns out wrong and then the father is praised when the children are good."

"I hear you."

"This one that Obi is warning me not to touch Junior, if eventually he turns out bad, he will blame me o, he won't remember my warning then."

"I still believe you have nothing to worry about, Nkechi."

But even as she said this, Ada knew it was not entirely true. There was always going to be a hint of worry and that uncertainty. But in the midst of it, there would always be a spark of hope as well.

9

Adrian didn't know what to expect when he got to Pastor Matthew's home late that Friday night. All he knew was that Chiedu had called him and told him to meet him there for some discussions, and that Chika would be joining them as well. Chiedu had insisted he would not take no for an answer since Adrian could not make it over to his place the day the pastor had visited.

When he got to the five-bedroom detached house at the Old G.R.A. Ikeja, an uneasiness flushed down his body leaving him cold. It was a beautiful white house with well-tended lawns and a set of exotic cars – a Mercedes, a BMW SUV, a Honda Civic and a Jaguar all parked alongside a huge satellite. He could not explain why he was feeling apprehensive, but he kept having sporadic flashes of another priest who had baptized him many years before. He visualized the white garment, burly dark figure and hairy arms. But that was not Pastor Matthew. Pastor Matthew was light-skinned with thick black hair that looked processed. He was not a tall man, neither was he big. He never wore white robes, only designer suits and expensive shirts and accessories. The most distinguishing thing Adrian could remember of Pastor Matthew was the nasal American inflection in his voice when he preached. It was quite easy to believe while listening to his sermons that the congregation was in faraway Harlem, New York, in one of those black Pentecostal churches with screaming, wildly gesticulating pastors who warned of impending doom, hell fire and brimstone.

Adrian noticed Chiedu's car as he made his way to the main entrance of the house. The car was parked close to the back gate of the compound. He had a quick look around to see if Chika's car was also there, but did not see it.

"Good evening, sir," a young man greeted him when he got to the entrance of the house.

"Hello," Adrian replied. "I'm here to see Pastor Matthew."

The young man led the way into the expansive and well-furnished lobby. Adrian eyed the various pictures hanging on the walls that captured the pastor's many trips to Europe and America on various crusades. Also on the walls were what seemed to be numerous awards or citations from foreign Christian institutes. Then there were the pictures of Pastor Matthew healing the sick and the crippled, the blind and the broken. Adrian found himself shuddering. He didn't feel right being here.

The young man motioned Adrian into what seemed to be a waiting room.Adrian entered the room and, to his relief, Chiedu was there, sitting by the window and reading a Bible. The man who brought Adrian up to this point bowed slightly and departed.

"Ebele," Chiedu said, closing the Bible, "how far?"

"I'm all right," Adrian replied. "Why are we meeting here?"

"Pastor Matthew would like to have a word with you."

Adrian noticed how Chiedu avoided eye contact with him and this further made him suspicious.

"Did you tell him that I'm gay?"

"Em…em… let's not talk about that issue."

Adrian shrugged indifferently and joined Chiedu on the seat. Despite their closeness on the couch, a thick wall separatd them. Chiedu went back to reading his Bible; at least it seemed he was reading it, with the silent movement of his lips. He continued to avoid looking directly at Adrian. Adrian wouldn't have minded much but, considering that it was Chiedu who invited him here anyway, he found it very annoying to be ignored. Just as he was about to voice his dissatisfaction, he sensed a presence. It was more of a strong body odour that remained offensive and dominant in spite of an attempt to mask it with an equally overwhelming cologne. Adrian looked up and was greeted by a smile from Pastor Matthew.

The pastor stood there with what Adrian believed to be a stupid grin on his face. His yellow bleached skin shimmered from the sweat that covered his face, and sweat stains left dark patches in the armpit area of his shirt. He was wearing a light blue shirt tucked into a pair of dark blue trousers with the sleeves rolled up. He wore a pair of alligator skin shoes.

"Good evening, Pastor." Chiedu rose up and shook hands with the pastor. "Thank you for seeing us this evening."

"Brother Chiedu!" Pastor Matthew shook his hand.

"Good evening, Pastor." Adrian said out of respect rather than conviction.

"Ah, Adrian!" the pastor said, squeezing Adrian's hand in turn. "It is good you came tonight. The Holy Ghost spoke to me about you."

Adrian was overwhelmed by his smell forcing him to take short breaths so as to avoid inhaling a full dose. He noticed that two stocky men lurked not too far away behind the pastor; they looked like bodyguards.

The image of the two men made Adrian think again

about his baptism. These two men were nothing like clergymen. They were sinister. One had a deep etching that ran across the right side of his face. It looked like someone had tried carving his face with a machete some time in the past. There was nothing holy about him.

"My dear brother," the pastor said, "sometimes we let the devil come into our lives and rule our hearts. And it's the evil deeds of Sodom and Gomorrah that made the Lord destroy the city and people of that place."

Adrian didn't know what to say. A part of him felt like laughing out loud, another part was angry and disappointed with his brother for making him suffer this indignity.

"When Brother Chiedu told me about you, I immediately got on my knees and prayed for you, and God told me that you would be saved and cured. It is the devil that tempts you my brother."

"Pastor…"

"Pray with me!" Pastor Matthew screamed, cutting Adrian short. "Close your eyes my brother and pray with me for God's mercy and strength."

Adrian tried to protest but felt the strong hands of the two burly men behind the pastor seize and pin him to the floor. It happened so fast and so unexpectedly that Adrian did not have a chance to react. When he realized what was happening he tried struggling, but his voice was already drowned out by the fervent praying of the pastor and the accompanying "amen" coming from his brother and the two men that held him down.

Things began to move even faster. The crescendo of the prayer rose as the pastor began speaking in tongues. Adrian cringed in horror. He felt his shirt being ripped off his body, rendering the upper part of his body naked. He watched in disbelief as the pastor withdrew a long five-pronged whip from behind one of the chairs and headed for him. Adrian struggled with more force and almost succeeded in freeing himself, but the two men pushed him down and tackled his arms in such a way that they almost dislocated his shoulder.

"Chiedu," Adrian screamed, "make them stop this madness… Chiedu…!"

Adrian noticed Chiedu's eyes were shut tightly in prayer. He kept on muttering "amen" and was oblivious to Adrian's plea. By now, raw fear had seized Adrian. His eyes focused on the menacing, approaching figure of the pastor who wielded the whip with vehemence and fanaticism.

When Pastor Matthew got close enough to Adrian, he raised the hand that held the whip and began muttering some gibberish. Adrian closed his eyes tightly and kept saying to himself, "I don't believe this is happening. I don't believe this is happening…"

Then there was the first sharp and searing lash of the whip on his bare back. It was an unbelievable pain, going straight to Adrian's head and making him suck in his breath sharply. He ground his teeth tightly and tried writhing away from the hands that bound him to the floor. With the next lash, his eyes flew wide open and he cried out in an agonizing shrill that momentarily startled the pastor who was in the motion of whipping him again. But the pause was just momentary, as the pastor continued in his mad fervour.

Stroke after stroke, Adrian sensed himself drifting in and out of consciousness. Sometimes he felt the pain of the whip when it licked his torso and ripped open a patch of flesh. Other times he drifted off with no sense of coherence. In his subconscious, he saw Christ in his passion, suffering in the hands of the Jews as they tortured his frail body.

"Banish the devil from your heart!" the pastor was screaming, "and accept God in your life."

"Amen, amen!" the others cried.

"The flesh is the Lord's temple, keep it clean and holy…"

Adrian faintly heard all this. His entire being was focused only on the numbing pain that spread itself across his body. At the moment when he thought it was over for him and he would give up, the beatings stopped. He was dimly aware of another set of arms that grabbed and carefully dragged him away to another corner. He heard a brief argument and what seemed to be threats and swearing. Slowly, he forced his eyes open and, just before he passed out, recognized Chika who was holding him tenderly with a worried look on his face.

Adrian remembered smiling weakly before finally letting the darkness overtake him.

◎ ◎ ◎

WHEN HE came to, Adrian was in a bedroom on a very soft bed. He was lying face down on the bed so his scarred and swollen back was exposed. He felt a balmy sensation on his back and could smell the pungent scent of a healing ointment that had been rubbed on his wounds.

His eyes were drawn to the bed sheets. The smooth linen sheets had an endless pattern of crimson-wine coloured roses that made Adrian think of blood. His blood. He closed his eyes for an instant as he vividly remembered the ordeal he had just experienced. He moved his right hand and slowly touched his sides. He winced at the pain. Pulling his hand back to examine it, he was not surprised to see traces of blood and the ointment smeared on his fingertips.

Slowly and painfully, he shook his head in disbelief. He had always suspected that Pastor Matthew was mad, but this just proved it to him. But as much as he would love to single out the pastor as an object of hatred, he knew that his reaction to Adrian's sexuality, was commonplace in their society. Adrian asked himself whether it was logical to despise an entire society because it looked down on his type. He so wanted to hate every single heterosexual person now. He wondered also whether it was right for a church to exhibit such hostility towards people like himself, when the same church was supposed to foster love, tolerance and understanding. He wondered, lastly, how his own brother could allow such a thing happen to him. It was this that hurt him the most, the devastating knowledge that his own flesh and blood had betrayed him. If he could not trust his elder brother, whom else could he trust?

Adrian heard a creaking noise from his left side and, as he turned, observed Chika entering the room carrying a bowl of water and some towels. He had a small smile on his face.

"Hey! How are you feeling?"

"My body hurts," Adrian confessed. He tried sitting up but found that the action itself caused him more pain.

"Relax." Chika sat on the side of the bed close to Adrian. "You have some terrible bruises. I will clean up the wound with warm water here."

He showed Adrian the bowl.

"There's some Dettol in the water so it may sting a bit, okay?"

Adrian nodded. He braced himself anxiously as Chika soaked one of the towels in the water, withdrew the wet towel, squeezed the excess liquid out and then placed the towel on his back with some pressure. He sucked his teeth as sharp needlelike pains surged through his body.

"I'm so sorry," Chika said quietly.

"It was not your fault, Chika."

"I suspected Chiedu might do something like this but I never believed it would go this far." Chika sighed. "I should have warned you… I should have been there earlier."

"You are here now."

The brothers stopped speaking, while Adrian endured Chika's effort to clean his wounds with the warm wet towel. He listened to the swooshing sound the water in the bowl made when Chika dipped his hands into it. He felt a bit better when Chika finally dried his back and then applied a soothing ointment to it as well.

"What happened?" Adrian asked.

"I was afraid something like that was going to happen so I had to get a friend of mine to follow me to Pastor Matthew's house, just in case. That was why I was late getting there. I was more than shocked when I saw what they were doing to you. My friend and I grabbed you and I threatened to call the police if they attempted to give us any trouble."

"And Chiedu?"

Chika shook his head sadly.

"I know he didn't mean you any harm," Chika said. "He's just finding it hard to accept your…"

"My homosexuality," Adrian completed his statement. "And what about you, do you accept it?"

Chika paused. He avoided Adrian's eyes and busied himself briefly by folding the unused towel and clearing away the things he had just used to treat Adrian's back. He dropped the bowl of water on the nearby dresser, as well as the ointment and used towels.

"Chika," Adrian said as he grabbed his hand, "why won't you answer me?"

"What do you want me to say?"

"Just tell me the truth. Do you accept me the way I am?"

Chika sighed uncomfortably and said, "The truth, Ebele, is that I don't understand why you are gay. We all came from the same home and background and share a similar childhood so it's hard to understand why you are this way. Truthfully, I wish you were not gay because I don't understand how you can be. I don't know what went wrong. But that's just my saying. It doesn't mean I will not stand by you and support you if this really is who you are."

Adrian considered what he had just said and a smile played across his lips. It wasn't that he found what Chika said funny; it was rather insightful. No one would ever understand how three bothers could be so different. No one would understand how, if they shared the same childhood and background, one could be gay. But that was just it. In that lay the answer to all their questions. They could all share the same background, home or memories, they could even be twins or triplets and one of them could still turn out gay, because that was the way it just was. He was simply who he was and always had been from the moment he was aware of himself. Why was this so hard for everyone else to see and accept?

"Thank you for telling me this."

Chika shrugged slightly and squeezed Adrian's hand, which he still held lovingly. He wished he could have been more positive and liberal-minded about his brother's sexuality but that was the best he could offer. When he looked at the welts on Adrian's back he remembered many years before when he had seen similar scars on his brother's back. When his brother had taken a punishment for him.

"Why did you do it?" Chika asked.

"Do what?" Adrian asked, bewildered.

"When we were kids, there was that time I took money from dad's room and you allowed yourself to be punished for it."

"Oh that."

"Why did you?" Chika desperately wanted to know. He

had waited for what seemed like a lifetime to understand why Adrian had done that.

"I didn't do it for you, silly!" Adrian laughed. "I was trying to tell Dad that I offered to return the money on your behalf before he quickly assumed I was the thief. After that, nothing mattered. Dad was always alive when he played with you. He loved you so much. I was afraid that if he had beaten you that night everything would change and he would never be the same again. I needed things to be the same."

"I don't understand that."

"I wanted things to be the same, you know."

"You wanted dad to continue loving me, so that he could remain alive!" Chika said in wonder. "And what about you?"

Adrian shrugged and finally sat up.

"You think dad hated you when we were kids?"

"Truth is, I was not the ideal son."

"They loved us all, you know," Chika said. "In different ways."

"I'm sure they did." Adrian's words lacked conviction.

Chika got up from the bed. He took the bowl, ointment and towels from the dresser and made for the entrance. He stopped by the door and looked back at Adrian.

"Mum is in the living room," he said. "Would you mind if she came in to see you?"

"Does she know?"

"Yes."

"If she wants to come, then let her come," Adrian said this though he knew he dreaded what may transpire.

When Chika left the room Adrian got up as well and raised his arms up in a stretch. It wasn't very successful as his back was on fire. He settled instead for pacing round the room. It wasn't a large space. There was a bed, a small dresser with a life-size mirror, a small, fourteen-inch television set in one corner and an adjoining bathroom. The room was carpeted all round. The rug was red as well, just like the roses on the sheets.

Adrian's back was to the door when his mother entered the room. He turned round to look at her as soon as he was aware of her presence. She was still beautiful. She had aged but traces of her beauty remained. Her face was still smooth and there was only a faint trace of ageing lines on the sides of her eyes and laugh lines on the sides of her mouth. Her hair on the other hand was more yellow-gray than anything he could remember. It was stretched in a perm and she had it packed to the back of her head and held in place with an ivory clasp. Adrian's mother stared at him with calm eyes. Her movements were subtle and careful. It was as if she was afraid to upset the equilibrium of the moment. She studied him as he studied her; they were like two strangers meeting for the first time.

"How are you?" The question was tentative.

"I'm fine, mum."

"What about your back?"

Adrian made a helpless gesture

His mother walked behind him and touched him when she was close enough, gently placing a finger on one of the fresh scars on his back. Adrian let her feel him. He could not remember when last her hands had touched him. His memory of that had long been suppressed, along with many other memories from the past.

"Is it painful?"

"Yes."

"Sorry," she said inadequately.

She withdrew her hand and slowly walked around to his front so she could see his face. Adrian at once noticed the build-up of tears in her eyes, and he felt her will herself not to let the tears roll down.

"What about dad?" Adrian asked. "Is he here?"

She shook her head and said: "He wouldn't come. He doesn't want to see you."

"I see," Adrian sighed and turned away.

"Ebele, why are you doing this to us?"

"What am I doing, mum?"

Adrian turned back so that his eyes could hold hers. Though his heart was beating fiercely, afraid of what she might say, he wanted to hear it all the same.

"We didn't bring any of you up like this," she cried. "We instilled in you all strong Christian values. What do you want people to think about our family?"

"What people will think?" Adrian repeated. "Is that what you care about the most? What about me? What do you care about me?"

"Ebele," his mother pleaded, "bikó, consider what news like this will do to our family. Your father's health is failing and this will surely kill him. When Chiedu told us about this, your father became so upset. His blood pressure went up and we had to even take him to the hospital. What about Ada and Ego? Have you considered what this will do to them? For once, stop thinking of yourself only."

In spite of himself, Adrian laughed bitterly. The chuckling noise rose from the base of his throat sounding cynical, cold and comical all at once.

"Mum, all I have done all my life is think about other people. If I had thought about myself alone then maybe all this would have been avoided. I'm not hurting you or anyone. I have only hurt myself by lying to myself."

She was weeping into her hands as he spoke and carefully lowered herself on the bed.

"What did we do wrong with you?" She said more to herself. "We tried to harden you when we noticed you were weak… We did everything to make you normal."

"Is that what you always thought?" Adrian asked. "That I was not normal."

Silence. Only her muffled sobs could be heard.

"Is that why you ignored me as a child?" Adrian's voice was raised. "Did you even love me, mum? Did dad ever love me?"

"We loved you the only way we knew how."

"But not as much as your beloved Chiedu or cherished Chika," Adrian added.

"What?"

"Mum," Adrian said, "please tell me something."

She looked at him expectantly, her eyes red and swollen with her grief.

"Do you agree with what happened to me tonight?" He asked. "Do you support what Chiedu and Pastor Matthew did to me?"

He kept his eyes on her, watching her squirm and writhe her hands nervously. She wasn't looking at him any more but at herself. She struggled to say something but it was obvious she was lost for words.

"What Chiedu did wasn't necessary," she finally said. "He is only worried about you."

Adrian smiled at this response and shook his head with self-pity. He looked around the room for his shirt but remembered the pastor's goons had ruined it. He noticed a shirt that had been laid out on the stool beside the bed. He approached the stool, grabbed the shirt and put it on carefully so as not to scratch his bruised back. He needed to leave this place. He was not happy with what he had heard. He wasn't expecting a miracle, like having his family accept him for who he was or embrace him and proclaim how much they cherished and loved him; no, he was not that ambitious. But he had not expected this either. He had not expected to learn that his parents thought he was not normal. They believed he was weak. They had always known he was different and that could be one of the reasons they could never show him love the way they ought to have when he was a child. He was awed by this knowledge. And he was hurt more deeply than he could have ever imagined or guessed.

"I have to go, mum."

He grabbed his car keys from the dresser and his mobile phone.

"Where are you going to?"

"I'm going away," he said coldly. "I need to go somewhere where I can think."

"What is wrong with staying here and thinking here? At least stay and listen to Chika."

"I can't!" Adrian said.

"Why?"

"Mother, I am a grown man," Adrian asserted. "I don't need an excuse to stay or go. I just can't stay here."

"What about your back?"

"It will heal. Goodbye mum."

He left her in the room, not sure if she was still crying for him or not. Chika was in his living room. He was sitting in his favourite corner close to his mini-library, facing a mute television set, deep in thought. A quietness had wrapped itself round him; Adrian felt he had no right to disturb this peace. But Chika had heard his light footsteps and turned to look at him.

"How far? Where's mum?"

"She's in the room."

"Where are you going?"

"Chika, I have to go. Thanks for everything."

"Where will you go? What will you do now?"

"I'll be okay. And I still have some things to sort out."

"Let me know if you need anything," Chika said.

"Thanks," Adrian smiled, "I will remember that."

Just as Adrian turned round and began walking away, he heard Chika say: "I love you, bro… Take care."

Adrian stopped.

"What did you say?"

"I said, take care," Chika said.

"No, before that."

Chika hesitated. "I said I love you, bro."

Adrian moved back to the living room where Chika now stood. Without warning he hugged him and as Chika hugged back, hot tears flowed down Adrian's cheeks. He let himself cry without holding back.

In his heart he had an overwhelming feeling of joy and happiness and yet he could not stop the tears from coming. All his life he had waited for a moment like this, when someone from his family would say those very words to him. And with Chika saying them, Adrian did feel lighter in his heart. He knew then that he would be all right and that it didn't matter what anyone thought about him, what he would cherish and keep was the knowledge that in this world of hate, prejudice and pain there were still people who loved him. People like his good friends Abdul, Femi and George; people like his brother Chika.

Even as he drove on the empty streets of Lagos that night, Adrian could not stop himself from smiling. He did not think of the pain in his back. He did not even think of what Chiedu had let happen to him. Nor did he remember the anger he had harboured for his parents for the way they had treated him as a child, the same anger that once ate at him, devouring his inside like a cancer. He smiled, knowing it was so easy to laugh or cry. He smiled because he knew it was equally undemanding to forgive and forget and then move on.

10

It was so appropriate that he had chosen the beach for them to meet. During their courtship, they spent a lot of time at Tarkwa Bay. She remembered how nervous she used to get at the jetty just by the American embassy. She hated the water and her palms used to get all sweaty and she actually trembled. Adrian would laugh and tell her to hold his hand, that everything would be all right. He said it with so much sincerity and love in his eyes, and with a spirited laugh. On the ferry he always kept his word, staying close and holding her until they got to the island beach. After many visits she overcame her fear of the water and could sit through the entire ferry ride without support or anxiety.

They had their spot at the beach. It was under two almost intertwining palm trees. A wrecked canoe lay half buried under these palms. Adrian and Ada would sit in this wreckage, shielded by the sun and away from other visitors who were strolling barefoot by the waterfront, letting the encroaching water cover their naked feet and soak up the wet, pale white sand.

Ada found her way to the spot and breathed a sigh of relief when she found their old boat was not occupied. Before she climbed into the boat she rushed to one of the trees and searched for the marking they had both made years earlier. It was a silly moment, like a Hollywood movie and fairytale-like she had remarked, but Adrian had gone ahead to inscribe two interlocking heart shapes on one of the trees and beneath it had scrawled: Ada and Adrian together forever. The etchings were still there. Ada smiled.

She got into the boat and tried to think more about the last couple of weeks. It had not been easy for her but she had lived through the worst moments. She had summoned up enough courage to face her parents and tell them she would be leaving her husband. Surprisingly there had not been that much of objection from either of them. Her two sisters were there, as well as her brother, and all the while they had remained strangely quiet and attentive. She could not tell them the real reason she was leaving Adrian; she didn't know how to get the words out of her mouth but, from the look in their eyes, Ada knew they must have heard about her husband's sexuality. It was in their eyes but they had been polite enough not to say anything about it, knowing it would embarrass her. There had been a hint of mad anger in her father's eyes, but not directed at her. Her mother had listened quietly with pity. Ada had known then that her marriage to Adrian would simply be forgotten and erased from their collective memories as if it had never happened. It would be relegated to the dark corner of their minds where all the unspoken taboos lay hidden. Taboos like Aunty Chichi's abortion, which she had when she was only sixteen, or Uncle Uche's illegitimate son who was now a big doctor in America. The knowledge of her homosexual husband would now be one of the family's dirty secrets and all would be forbidden to breathe a word of it.

Then there was the issue of their daughter, Ego. Her parents had offered to raise Ego so she could have two parents, but Ada thanked them and rejected the offer. She would care for her child and Adrian too would have access to her as well. She wasn't going to deny him his rights. She wasn't going to estrange Ego from her father.

In her way she had made peace with herself and situation. She no longer felt sorry for herself; neither did she feel ashamed as if she had brought all of it on herself. She had learnt to accept that unfortunate things happen to good people every day. Some married couples would always stay married while some split up. She would not be the first woman to walk away from a marriage that was not meant to last forever. She was at peace with this knowledge at last.

It helped that she had been visiting with Carol and the other ladies, Hajiya and Temi. Finally she had found a comfort zone with these ladies. She got to understand the reason for their indifference and attitude. It was their way of protecting and shielding their already fragile hearts. With these ladies she learnt how to laugh again and live. It was strange how she now looked forward to her weekly meeting with them, she who had once despised what she believed they stood for.

"Hey you!"

Ada looked up and Adrian was standing over her, backing the sun, wearing a pair of white linen trousers and a flowing patterned shirt that was unbuttoned to his navel. He looked absolutely handsome.

"Adrian!" Ada stood up and hugged him. It was their first body contact since she learnt of his secret past.

Adrian joined her in the canoe. He sat opposite her. He seemed calm and relaxed.

"So, how have you been?"

"I'm fine, Ada."

"And your back?" Chika had told her about what happened at the pastor's house.

"It's been two weeks now. I have healed nicely."

"I'm glad for you."

"Thank you."

They looked into each other's eyes and then away to the waves of the beach, then back at each other again.

"How have you been?" Adrian asked.

"I'm fine."

"And Ego?"

"She's fine. You talk to her every day."

"Good...good," Adrian said, clasping his hands. "What about us?"

"Adrian, I think you know what we must do."

"Divorce?"

Ada nodded slowly. "We can't continue to be married. Or do you want us to?"

Adrian sighed. "I suppose you are right. We should divorce and get on with our lives."

Ada shifted uneasily. Having him confirm the inevitability of their separation made her feel a deep sense of loss. She knew it was the only thing to do, the only thing she could agree to in the circumstances.

"I worry about Ego though. How do we explain all this to her?"

"She is just a child and very soon will stop asking questions. When she is older we can tell her something."

"She will want to know the truth then."

"Then we tell her the truth. I will make sure she is brought up with love and tolerance so she doesn't discriminate against people irrespective of their beliefs and lifestyle."

She was telling him that their daughter would have to learn eventually that her father was gay, and she would have to make her own choice to either accept or disassociate herself from him. She would make sure that Ego respected Adrian as her father always. This was a promise she had made to herself.

"Will you remarry?"

"I don't know if I will," Ada said truthfully. "I have not had any time to consider that... Why do you ask?"

"I don't know," Adrian shrugged, "I was only thinking of Ego having another father. I guess I would be jealous, but I don't want you to be lonely for the rest of your life as well."

Ada smiled. She was touched by his words. He still cared enough to worry about her loneliness.

"I need to know, Adrian," Ada said, "did you ever truly love me?"

"Yes, I did. I still do."

"But you are gay."

"Yes, I am."

"How can you love a woman?" Ada asked. "Doesn't that contradict with your sexuality?"

"What is your understanding of gay?" Adrian countered.

"I don't know," Ada shrugged again. "Two people of the same sex having sex."

Adrian smiled at her and shook his head in mock exasperation. He had known that was going to be her answer.

"You shake your head. What is it then?"

Adrian paused momentarily to gather his thoughts. He had to look for the right words to explain to her what it truly meant to be gay.

"I have come to learn," he began, "that being gay has nothing to do with the physical action of sex or a person's sexual preference, be it with the opposite sex or same sex. Sleeping with a man or woman will always remain the individual's choice. I am gay because it is who I am. It is the way I see the world. It is the way I reason and live. It is waking up in the morning and going to bed at night. It is listening to music and loving it. It is watching a movie and wanting to see it over again. It is laughing when I am happy and crying when I am sad. It is appreciating the simple things life brings and not the act of sexual intercourse. Sex on its own is a physical expression of love or lust. I could love a woman because of the qualities she possesses and still be gay. A man can be gay all his life without actually sleeping with another man. Can you understand this?"

"I don't know, Adrian," Ada confessed, "I don't know if I can understand anything you have just said. It is asking me to disregard all I have learnt all my life. It is asking me to put aside all the Bible's teachings and accept your word only. I've promised myself not to judge you or your kind because I would never really understand why you are the way you are and I will make sure our daughter is not prejudiced either."

"Okay, Ada, I'm not trying to convert you to my way of thinking but I want you to understand me a little better. I want when you think about me not to see a monster who deceived you but a man who loves you."

"I know… I know," Ada said. "What about you? What do you intend to do with yourself?"

"I really don't know. I get back to work on Monday and I have to decide if I want to continue there or move to another company. I have even thought about relocating to another country."

"Relocating?"

"I'm a realist, Ada," Adrian sighed. "Nigeria is not tolerant of my kind and I want to work and live in a place where I won't have to deny my sexuality. If I'm asked 'Are you gay?' I want to answer truthfully, 'Yes, I am.' If I remain here, I will always be a victim. I will always have to worry about what the next person is thinking about me or that I may lose my job at any time or not get the necessary recognition I deserve at work."

"If you leave, what about Ego and me?" Ada asked.

"How would we get to see you?"

"I haven't made up my mind on anything yet," Adrian smiled warmly. "But whatever I do, even if I do relocate, I will make sure both of you will always have contact with me."

"God! This is depressing talk. Let's not talk about going away and relocating. Let us talk about happy things."

"That's funny," Adrian laughed. "I remember you telling me not long ago that you had nothing to say to me…"

"Oh stop it!" Ada slapped his knee playfully. "I was angry then and in shock, you know."

"So what has changed now?"

"It was something you said some time ago. You said you were still the same person and it is true. You are still you. And then I began to question myself after Nkechi told me she feared that her son could be gay. She wouldn't love him less if he were, neither would I. So I had to ask myself why I could not accept you the way you are."

"I see," Adrian said thoughtfully.

She hoped he did. He was smiling and she smiled back. This had turned out better than she had hoped. They would remain friends and would not have to squabble about who had custody of their daughter. He had also opened up to her about deep issues regarding his sexuality. She did not know what to make of it, but somehow she understood his frustrations.

The wind was blowing with a bit more force now and she had to use her hand to brush her hair from her face. They both looked up at the sky as if they expected rain but there was no grey cloud in sight. Looking back at each other with laughing eyes, an unspoken pact passed between them; that, no matter what, for the rest of their lives they would always be open and honest with each other and they would always be friends.

◎ ◎ ◎

THIS WAS something he should have done many years earlier, he kept telling himself. If he had had the courage to confront this moment all those years past, maybe things would have turned out differently. Maybe fewer people would have been hurt by his actions.

He felt like he had returned home. In fact it was like he had never left the sprawling one-acre estate, the winding road that led from the gate to the mansion, the expansive green lawns and flower gardens with palm trees that gave the property character. He remembered so well the stable at the back that housed three-prized stallions and a little riding field. He remembered the pool and servant quarters that were utilized by the cook Famous, the driver Adamu and the gardener Jacob. This used to be his second home so long before. He vividly remembered hanging around or throwing small dinner parties by the pool during long lazy weekends with his close male friends.

But in these memories, there had always been Antonio. If it could be said that Adrian had only truly loved once in his lifetime, that love would have been Antonio. He had been happiest with him. They had met when the Spanish embassy threw a dinner for all Spanish nationals and companies that had business interests in Nigeria. Adrian's firm was an affiliate of a Spanish multimedia conglomerate. He had attended the dinner reluctantly. He sat on the same table as Antonio and in the course of the evening, they got to know a little about each other. It was obvious to both of them that the other was gay. They exchanged cards and numbers and thus began their brief friendship, which quickly became a more intimate affair.

It was a wonderful period for Adrian until the moment when he was betrayed. He never thought it possible to feel that much hurt, neither did he know how much he had let himself love Antonio. Prior to meeting Antonio he had never considered that he could be content in a relationship with another man, and this was largely due to the negative perceptions people had of things like that. But it happened and he got burnt.

He was seated now in the beautifully furnished lounge. It was more beautiful than he remembered it. There must have been several redecorations over the years, as Adrian observed a couple of pieces that had not been there when he last visited the house. It had a retro feel; the black leather seats contrasting the white marble flooring, the metallic entertainment unit against a backdrop of clear glass, and Chinese lamps hanging from the high ceiling.

Adrian was offered a drink but declined politely. He was told that Antonio was taking a shower and would be joining him in the next couple of minutes. He smiled his understanding as the young manservant retreated to the kitchen. As soon as he was alone again, he got up and walked over to the display shelves next to the entertainment unit. There was a framed picture of himself and Antonio on the top shelf. They had taken that picture when they holidayed together in Brighton. Antonio had his arm playfully round Adrian's neck in a chokehold and they were both smiling. It was one of the most memorable times they had spent together.

"I remember you said you wanted that moment to last forever and I said I would make sure it did."

Adrian turned round to face Antonio. He looked lean. His wild curly hair that Adrian remembered with such fondness was now cut really low. But he still had an irresistible sparkle in his big, honey-brown eyes and a mischievous curve to his lips when he smiled.

"Adrian, my Adrian," Antonio said. "What a pleasant

surprise and you look great, I must add."

"Antonio," Adrian replied, "you look...different."

"Darling, my age is catching up with me, you know."
He moved close to Adrian and embraced him fondly. "How
come you don't have a drink? Isaac!" he shouted for his
manservant.

"It is okay," Adrian stopped him. "I was offered but
refused. I'm okay."

Antonio looked at him comically and then shrugged.

"Come now." Antonio beckoned to him. "Come join
me on the couch and talk to me. To what do I owe this visit?
I thought I ranked with the devil in your books."

Adrian sat on the couch, leaving a small space between
them that could have taken another person. It felt strange
being this close to Antonio but it was a new kind of
strangeness. Adrian did not feel apprehensive, nor did his
heart flutter with love or excitement like it would have
years earlier. He just felt superior at that moment, superior
because he had been able to survive without Antonio for all
those years and also conquer the anger.

The betrayal and anger he had harboured for so long
had blinded him and made him despise himself and his
sexuality. He had questioned God in his prayers, why He
had made him the way he was. He cursed himself for being
different. But he could not be any other way. Just like he
had told Ada, being gay was everything about him and not
just the sexual act itself.

"So, talk to me," Antonio cooed, "what has been
happening to you?"

"I'm getting a divorce," Adrian said. "And I'm moving
to London."

"Wow!" Antonio exclaimed. "Those are big steps. What
about your job?"

"I qualify as a highly skilled immigrant, so I have work

waiting for me already in the U.K.," Adrian explained. "I just wanted to see you before I leave and tell you that I am no longer angry. I don't hate you."

Antonio spoke softly. "Thank you, that means a lot to me."

"You seem sad. Are you okay?"

Antonio looked away into the distance. There was a far-away look in his brown eyes that momentarily fluttered, and then he smiled warmly.

"I am HIV-positive, Adrian."

Adrian felt the wind knocked out of his lungs. He stared hard at Antonio, searching his lean but handsome face for a sign that he was only joking, that he was playing one of his cruel jokes on him. But this was not funny and Adrian feared that it was also the truth.

"Is this true?"

"Yes."

"When did you find out?"

"June last year."

"How come?" Adrian asked. "How did you get it? You always told me to play safe. When we were together we always used protection."

"I know," Antonio said, "but I got careless after you left me. Too many beautiful black men, so little time…"

"Don't joke with something like this," Adrian cried. "You are going to die, Antonio, don't you realize that?"

"Good news for homosexuals, heterosexuals die too. You shouldn't take this so seriously. I'm okay and getting treatment."

"This is a serious thing, Antonio," Adrian repeated, "you are going to die."

"Yes, eventually. But so will you and every person alive today. We all will die of something eventually."

"I know this. But it could have been prevented. Because

I know that I will die of something some day does not mean I should run out into a busy highway and risk getting knocked down and killed… It is the same with sex."

"Okay, Adrian, stop the preaching. I didn't tell you I am HIV-positive to freak you out, I just thought you would have liked to know."

"Thank you for telling me," Adrian said after a long pause. "But are you okay? Is there anything I can do for you?"

"I'm good. And thanks for offering, but everything is under control. I have my medication and regular visits to my doctors. I can beat this."

"Okay, Antonio." Adrian stood up to go. "I'm happy it is under control but do take care. I will call on you before I leave for England."

They hugged again and Antonio kissed his cheeks before Adrian walked out of the lounge into the sun. His face was cast down, deep in thought, his eyes locked in a trance on his moving shadow. He would not have wished this for even his worst enemy. But Antonio had brought this on himself. He had chosen to have multiple partners and not use protection when it mattered most. This was a part of the reckless lifestyle of many gay men that bothered Adrian. He wondered why so many people thought nothing of having multiple partners, why some felt incomplete if they did not sample as many different people as possible. He was no saint himself. There had been a time he was like that, but he had believed he was trying his options to eventually find the right partner. That was what he told himself then, but he had to admit now that it was not quite true. Even in his reckless days, he had always known that there was no chance that Nigeria would evolve to allow same-sex unions, so finding a long-term partner could be emotionally risky, as it would never last. Moving on to the next partner had been his emotional trump card against disappointment. But even then he had been careful. He wondered briefly if this could be the reason for the rampant promiscuity within the gay community? But Adrian had long ceased searching for answers to these questions . Antonio's choices were his choices and his alone. Every man would have to live and die on his own terms. He was just glad that he had finally found some closure.

He had tried to erase from his memory his relationship with Antonio and had tried to pretend that he could lead what many termed a normal life with a wife, and the false sense of security it offered. But deep inside he knew that the only person he was fooling was himself. He had found some peace with Ada and Ego, but there had always been the nagging feeling that something in his life remained incomplete.

EPILOGUE

Ebele. Ebele Njoko. That was his name. It was who he was.

It felt so good when the uniformed lady at the check-in counter at the international airport studied his passport, smiled at him and casually said his name: Njoko Ebele Adrian. She looked at him in the eye briefly before dragging her eyes back to the picture on the passport. She said his name aloud as if to affirm that it was the very same person whose picture was on the passport that stood before her.

"It's Ebele Njoko," he said with ease. "Or simply Ebele."

"I kind of like the sound of Adrian, it is a beautiful name," the lady said, "but rather unusual for a Nigerian."

She handed him back his passport and boarding pass. As he moved away to have his luggage checked by the Nigeria Customs, he couldn't help but feel content with finally accepting himself for who he was. He had allowed Ebele to lie dormant for far too long, and now it was like a resurrection being addressed as Ebele by everyone once again.

It had certainly been a long and often gruelling journey for Adrian to get to this point in his life. Yes, he was leaving his home country to pursue new beginnings abroad, but he did not view this as running away. He had simply decided to move on with his life and remain true to himself. Unfortunately he would not be able to be himself if he remained in Nigeria. The majority of the people here still viewed his sexuality as abnormal. Maybe they were right, maybe they were wrong. Ebele simply knew he was the way he was right from the moment he became aware of himself as a human. No one had a right to judge him. But people would. He understood that. He could not hate them for this. Hating them would mean hating his father, mother and brothers. He could not hate people for not understanding him. Sometimes he did not understand himself either.

The Customs official who wasn't smiling returned his bags to him and Adrian handed them to the airline's baggage handler by the check-in counter. He looked at his watch and noted he still had an hour before the flight was due to take off. He decided to wait in the first class lounge and probably have a drink. He felt a tinge of abandonment and loneliness walking through the airport alone. No one had come to see him off that morning. He had wanted it that way, to depart quietly and without fanfare, and that was why he had chosen a weekday morning to travel. Everyone he knew had to be at work. He had spent some time with both Ada and Ego the day before and they all had a wonderful time. It was almost like the old days when they were a proper family. No, it had been even better than his memory of them as a family. They had talked like there was no tomorrow and truth was, there would be no tomorrow for a very long time. They laughed together and then cried some more.

The divorce had come through over a month before. It had gone smoothly with the lawyers. The reason given for their separation was 'irreconcilable differences' and they didn't have to go into any detailed account of the issues involved.

His in-laws, Ada's parents and her siblings, had remained

civil throughout the proceedings and the separation period. They had wanted nothing to do with him, which he could understand. Ada on the other hand was supportive and gracious. She made it clear to her family that she would not tolerate anyone attacking him. After they had signed the papers that would sever their marital ties, Ada could not stop her tears. She hugged him tightly and cried on his shoulder while he fought back his own tears. Ego had a bemused look on her face; she was still too young to understand what was going on. Eventually her face crumpled and she joined her mother in crying. He had wondered then what she would make of all this in years to come, when she would be old enough to understand why her parents had to split up. He only hoped that when that day came she would still love him and accept him and not hide in shame of him. Hopefully Nigeria would be a different place then and its people would be more receptive and less judgmental than they were now. He could only hope.

In the lounge, Adrian discreetly observed the cocktail of travellers who mingled about. He wondered how many of them were like him. How many of them were leaving behind a false life here to start anew in a foreign land? What kind of secrets did they all carry inside?

The attractive young lady sitting across from him smiled invitingly. She was dressed smartly and professionally in a gray suit. On the table in front of her was a tiny designer label bag and on her lap was an overcoat. She was not wearing any rings on her fingers.

"Hello!" She smiled as she greeted Adrian.

He replied politely before looking away, showing no interest.

He could only guess what thoughts ran through her mind as she looked at him. She probably was thinking; here was an attractive, young, unmarried man who looked cultured and who had the means to travel first class. She probably thought she could get along with him and flirt a little; after all, what was the harm in flirting? He wondered how she would react if he told her that he was gay, just like many other men out there who looked and acted masculine. Would she squeeze her pretty face in disgust and pull away instantly? She probably would. He laughed at the thought.

The final boarding announcement for his flight blared from the public address system overhead. He picked his hand luggage and made his way out of the lounge. It was a long walk to the gate. A mother and her son brushed past him. The child was humming a tune that was familiar to him.

Ringa-Ringa-Roses
A-Pocket-Full-of-Poises...

He felt a chill run down his spine as he recited the nursery rhyme in his head. He watched mother and child scurry off but he kept staring, long enough to see the boy turn back and stare right back at him with big vacant eyes.

He knew that boy. He recognized him. He used to be that boy when he was that same age. He remembered his fear. He remembered his confusion. But most of all he remembered the acute sense of loneliness that had surrounded him.

He was no longer that scared lonely child who did not understand why his father would not throw him up in the air and catch him. He no longer wondered why he could never enjoy the games his brothers played. He knew who he was now and he had found the acceptance he had once craved within himself.

Ebele became aware that his heart was racing fast, like he had just finished a hundred metre dash. He did not know if it was uncertainty he was feeling or a deep sense of sadness at the thought of leaving so much behind.

Whatever it was, one thing was certain: he was going away and in his new life he was determined to be happy, and nothing was going to make him afraid anymore.

AFTERWORD

When the anthology Camouflage: Best of Contemporary Writing from Nigeria was published last year I had no hesitation in claiming that "Nigeria is the powerhouse of African literature and here, in Camouflage, is the evidence."

Jude Dibia's two novels to date—Walking With Shadows and Unbridled—provide fresh evidence to strengthen such a claim. Worldwide, "third generation" Nigerian novelists such as Helon Habila, Chimamanda Ngozi Adichie, Sefi Atta and Chris Abani have grabbed the headlines (and the prizes) and Dibia deserves to join their ranks.

What is immediately striking about his work is his courage in tackling subject-matter that is, for one reason or another, generally avoided by other African writers and his mastery of characterization and plot, which makes his work exceptionally gripping. Beware—reading Dibia's novels may lead to sleep deprivation.

In the case of Walking With Shadows, the central character, Adrian, is head of the business risk unit in the Lagos office of a multinational company. And "risk" is a key term here, as he is also gay.

Dibia's is not, of course, the first Nigerian novel to feature a gay character; Soyinka broke new ground with his characterization of Joe Golder, the African-American homosexual in his 1965 novel The Interpreters. What is innovatory about Dibia's work is that the characterization of Adrian is not only insightful but also deeply sympathetic.

A married man, Adrian, has concealed his gay orientation from all but a small coterie of friends. As the novel opens, he is threatened with outing by a former employee, whose dismissal on charges of corruption he has been partly responsible for.

Ada, his wife, is the first to be told and much of the novel has to do with her and with Adrian's anguish in realizing that their marriage has run on to the rocks. Dibia cuts no corners here and his depiction of the marital crisis is very moving.

Adrian's relatives also learn the truth. There is a painful and inconclusive interview between Adrian and his mother, and while his younger brother attempts to reach out to him, the elder sibling subjects him to a brutal attempt at exorcism by an American-trained Pentecostal priest.

At one point Adrian protests to his brothers: "I didn't wake up this morning and decide to ruin everybody's life." Yet while Dibia makes it very clear how painful Adrian's dilemma is, moral considerations are also explored. Adrian's marriage has, after all, been strung across the chasm of a lie, like the most tenuous of rope bridges, and the suffering this causes Ada is her husband's doing.

The quality of Dibia's insight enables him to address a whole range of issues relevant to Adrian's crisis. There is, for example, the question of the contradictions that bedevil assumptions about culture and identity. While Ada, an interior designer, acknowledges the fact that much of the artwork and décor she admires challenges her concept of African cultural norms, she can't begin to accept same-sex sexuality as anything other than irredeemably alien.

Dibia is excellent at depicting Adrian's fears—which deepen into a vertiginous panic—as the news about him spreads. In one especially powerful episode, semi-ostracized by his boss and staff, he hallucinates a message on his computer screen:

THEYKNOWWHATYOUARE
THEYKNOWWHATYOUARE...

Throughout, Dibia focuses on the telling moment, the minutiae of consciousness. There is a lovely episode earlier, when the child Adrian stands under the balcony on which his father, fresh out of the bath, is combing his hair, believing that the drizzle that falls on him must be a shower of love.

Underlying all of this is the issue of identity and the question how an individual negotiates recognitions about the self. As a child, Adrian believes he must "reinvent himself" and purge himself of the "pathetic person" he and his brothers believe himself to be. Years later, he has a recurring dream of childhood, his parents waking him out of sleep and bringing him into the living-room to meet his real parents. Now, exposed, he has to muster all his courage, his internal resources, in order to weather the storm and to find a more honest, responsive and self-fulfilling way of living his life.

With this second edition of Walking With Shadows, Dibia has taken the opportunity to revise his text. This is a somewhat unusual venture, much more common when, say, individually published short stories or poems are gathered into a collection, though there is a significant precedent in Achebe's novel Arrow of God, which was first published in 1964 and appeared in a revised edition ten years later.

In his preface to that new edition, Achebe had this to say: "Arrow of God . . . is the novel which I am most likely to be caught sitting down to read again. On account of that I have also become aware of certain structural weaknesses in it which I now take the opportunity of a new edition to remove."

Dibia has corrected some grammatical flaws that crept into the first edition of Walking With Shadows, but he has also gone further in introducing an entirely new episode. Apart from its intrinsic value, this throws fresh light on the working procedures of the novelist.

The new episode has to do with one of the novel's most interesting and appealing characters, Rotimi, who is Adrian's subordinate at work and a staunch supporter of his boss, even when Adrian is stigmatized by his other colleagues. Rotimi tells Adrian he is not gay himself, but that he has once made love to a male friend. At a point, he attempts to kiss Adrian, who is so taken aback: he (gently) repels the advances.

In the original text, the incident is developed no further than this. Rotimi remains an enigma and we have no idea how the incident with Adrian might have affected him. The new episode, which is embedded in Chapter 7, fleshes out our sense of Rotimi's character, his ambiguous orientation and his not very successful attempts to examine his feelings for Adrian (as throughout the novel, an important theme here is "know thyself"). But—and this is admirable—Dibia doesn't attempt to minimize ambiguities or to tie up loose ends (for they cannot be tied up). It is rather that as readers we are now given more to go on, to feel our way into Rotimi's acutely difficult situation.

The inclusion of the new episode allows fresh insight into Dibia's remarkable conscientiousness in his handling of his materials, and into his lively creative intelligence.

Dibia's two novels to date—Walking With Shadows and Unbridled—make for compulsive reading and deserve the widest possible audience.

Chris Dunton
National University of Lesotho

Have You Read?

More by Jalaa Writers' Collective

PRIDE OF THE SPIDER CLAN
BY ODILI UJUBUONU

Odidika is exiled at the age of twelve. The forces that tiled his chequered history challenge him on land and at sea. His fight for freedom is not just against his enemies but includes himself. And he realises that the battle prize goes beyond a flute lost in the heart of *Izon* creeks...

Caught in the web of an old family quandary, Isikamdi arrives at the terminus of fate. Part of his choices is to die. Part is to live. The destiny of a people rests on this decision. The elements quake, the fauna and flora awaken and an arcane group of Aro men keenly awaits him.

The destiny of these two men and that of the entire Aro people collide on the stake of the sacred flute.

Pride of the Spider Clan, Odili Ujubuonu's third novel, is a

breathtaking interplay of seen and
unseen forces across the labyrinths
of the lower Niger. It is a story of
courage and commitment high on
regenerating the self, family and
society.

The mythical outpouring of Odili
Ujubuoñu's Pride *of the Spider Clan*
is seductive. Untying Odidika and
Isikamdi's shared fate with the
sacred *ofo* is heart thumping and
mind blowing
    ... These heroes must not fail.
– Nwachukwu Egbunike, Editor
Fast Edition and Feathers Project.

ROSES AND BULLETS
BY AKACHI ADIMORA-EZEIGBO

Roses and Bullets is the heart-rending story of Ginika and Eloka, two star-crossed lovers, whose love was halted and destroyed by the Biafran war and further complicated by other circumstances. The novel is also about their families and their relationships riddled with conflicts.

Roses and Bullets takes us right into the experience of war: its divisiveness, the pain caused by untimely and violent death, and the humanity that prevails in spite of pain and violence. It comes from a voice of experience, providing depth and insight into a traumatic period in Nigeria's life in a most moving, graphic way. In reading, we live a little along with the characters, sharing both the trauma and the hope of new life.

– **Pat Bryden,
Edinburgh, Scotland**

Printed in the USA
CPSIA information can be obtained
at www.ICGtesting.com
LVHW051944120124
768844LV00002B/118